He pointed out the door. "After you, Princess."

Princess. She was going to start laughing again, and this time she might not stop until she was crying. Or screaming. "There has been a mistake," she said firmly. The same way she'd spoken when she'd told Sophia she would take care of everything.

You've certainly taken care of things, Ilaria.

"Even if you don't like them, there has been one," she said before he could stop her. "Sophia told me she was meant to have dinner with a duke or a lord. I was only going to go through with the dinner, refuse the impending proposal, then go home to Accogliente and—"

"Silence."

Ilaria immediately clamped her lips together. It was as natural as breathing, following his sharp order.

"What exactly are you saying?" the prince demanded.

Still, she had to muster all her courage and set this to rights. Her heart pounded, and her hands shook even as she clutched them together. But she held his dark, intimidating gaze. "My name isn't Sophia. Sophia is my cousin. You've married the wrong woman."

Lorraine Hall is a part-time hermit and full-time writer. She was born with an old soul and her head in the clouds, which, it turns out, is the perfect combination to spend her days creating thunderous alpha heroes and the fierce, determined heroines who win their hearts. She lives in a potentially haunted house with her soul mate and rambunctious band of hermits-in-training. When she's not writing romance, she's reading it.

*This is **Lorraine Hall**'s debut book for Harlequin Presents—we hope that you enjoy it!*

Lorraine Hall

THE PRINCE'S ROYAL WEDDING DEMAND

Recycling programs for this product may not exist in your area.

ISBN-13: 978-1-335-73909-4

The Prince's Royal Wedding Demand

Harlequin Enterprises ULC
22 Adelaide St. West, 41st Floor
Toronto, Ontario M5H 4E3, Canada
www.Harlequin.com

Printed in U.S.A.

THE PRINCE'S ROYAL
WEDDING DEMAND

For Flo & the Ms

CHAPTER ONE

THIS WAS NOT the "simple dinner" Ilaria Russo had been expecting.

It was supposed to be straightforward. Pretend to be Sophia, her cousin, have a long, boring dinner with some lord or duke, and then when he inevitably proposed, turn him down.

All the while Sophia would be escaping and eloping with the man she really loved—a sailor her father did not approve of.

Giovanni Avida might be Ilaria's uncle—the man who'd married her late mother's sister—but Ilaria considered him one of her few enemies in life. His grasping, conniving accumulation of wealth had created terrible conditions at the mine her father had worked and subsequently been killed at. The disaster had taken the lives of not just her father, but twenty other men from her village.

And instead of receiving any punishment for his actions, Giovanni had been given a job in the King's ministry. Instead of helping his orphaned niece, he had refused to let Ilaria visit his home in wealthy Roletto.

The only "kind" thing he'd done was allow his wife to sometimes bring their daughter, Sophia, to Accogliente to visit Ilaria. Ilaria had always assumed it was the one thing her aunt insisted upon.

While Ilaria had maintained a close friendship with her sweet cousin, Giovanni had spent the past ten years amassing yet more wealth and influence, and desperately trying to get Sophia married off to a title so he could have one himself.

So, when given the opportunity to thwart *him* and help her sweet cousin who deserved escape from her father's ironclad control, Ilaria had taken it.

Now she was here in Roletto, the capital city of Vantonella, using her considerable likeness to Sophia to take her cousin's place.

While Ilaria was certain of her purpose, nerves had set in when she entered the sparkling city nestled between the towering European Alps and the shining Lago di Cornio. There were so many buildings. So many people bustling around the train station. She'd spent the entirety of her twenty-four years in the little cottage built by her ancestors centuries ago, deep in the Pecora mountain region of Vantonella, farming and sheep herding and helping her grandfather until his death last year.

She'd had a brief moment of panic in the train station when she'd considered turning around and running home, but Sophia and her sailor had found Ilaria in the crowd. Though Sophia had acted somewhat strange, they'd exchanged clothes, identification and hugs. Ilaria had wished her cousin well. The meeting with Sophia had returned most of her courage.

Until Ilaria had reached the address Sophia had provided and found an ancient cathedral instead of a restaurant. Until she'd been gestured inside by a soldier in full military regalia. Until she'd looked down the aisle to see a tall man in the shadows. Presumably waiting for her.

Something about the incredibly ornate altar made Ilaria very, *very* nervous. The soldier who'd opened the door and now stood there watching her did not help. She wiped her sweaty palms on the hips of her borrowed dress.

"Your purse," the soldier intoned, holding out a hand.

Ilaria looked down at the small purse she clutched. It was Sophia's, like everything she wore, and it felt wrong to give it up. The soldier did not seem impressed with Ilaria's hesitation, however, and Ilaria knew she had to do her best not to act like the country mountain girl she was.

For tonight, you are well-to-do, well-trained Sophia Avida. You will firmly turn down whatever marriage proposal is made here. And you will give Sophia the time to disappear, never to be found by her controlling, scheming father again.

Tomorrow, once she was certain that Sophia was married and safe, Ilaria would go home to her farm. She had left it in capable hands. After the mining disaster ten years ago, her grandfather had begun to hire orphan children to help tend the sheep. Ilaria had worked with him to create whatever opportunities they could for those children and their widowed mothers to stay in their home village, rather than be shipped off to orphanages and workhouses in the city and lose their homes on top of everything else they'd lost.

Because *that* had been the King's and her uncle's grand plan for disaster relief.

Ilaria and her grandfather had done what they could with tragedy. And now those children were coming into adulthood with a set of skills, and small savings, to rebuild their own lives. Those widows had been able to feel as though they'd taken good care of their children, even in a village with few financial opportunities outside generational farms, with the mine now shuttered.

It was not quite the same scale, but Ilaria liked to think that by stepping in to help Sophia, she was doing what her grandfather would have done. Given someone an alternative that would allow them freedom and happiness.

She had not been able to protect her father from the mining disaster. She had not been able to stop the slow decline in her grandfather's health that had ended with his passing last year. But she could save Sophia from a sad, manipulative life in the titled circles of Roletto.

"Sophia, please move forward," the shadowed man instructed from down the aisle.

Ilaria did so, compelled by the authoritarian voice. She had to swallow down the nerves, straighten her shoulders, and not wilt at the depth and certainty in the voice that beckoned her forward.

Down the long, intimidating aisle. She looked back once, but the soldier now stood in the middle of her exit. Like he was blocking it.

This is all wrong.

Still, she moved toward the man at the end of the aisle. *For Sophia. And, in a way, for Uncle Giovanni.*

Each footstep echoed in the grand marble building. Dim lights cascaded through bright stained glass, and gold and silver seemed to shine and glow everywhere she looked.

She'd never seen anything so opulent in her life. It likely rivaled the inside of the royal palace. She was used to patched roofs and muddy roads and the sound of farm animals in the distance.

As she reached the end of the aisle, she realized two terrifying truths at once. First, there was a second man here. Shorter in stature, standing behind a pulpit, a Bible opened in front of him.

Second, and more importantly, the man who'd beckoned her closer was not a duke or a lord.

He was *Prince* Frediano Montellero, the direct heir to the Vantonella throne.

Ilaria was sure she gaped up at him. Her shock had to be evident in every slack muscle on her face. Even in her small village she'd seen pictures of the famed Prince. The *heir*, who was nothing like his wild and impetuous parents who'd died at a young age *free*-climbing the intimidating Monte Morte.

Prince Frediano was said to be as proper and *honorable* as his grandfather, the great King Carlo. Ilaria had never understood how anyone could call the monarchy honorable when they gave schemers and all but murderers places in their ministries. When they were so out of touch with people in need that they suggested things like moving those who'd lost everything to cramped rooms and orphanages in the city.

That did not mean she was *immune* to her reaction at standing *next* to Prince Frediano, with his stunningly sculpted face, surprisingly broad soldiers and a dark suit that no doubt had cost more than her entire *life*. His hair was a glossy black, kept cropped short in such a way he gave the impression of some kind of *warrior*. No doubt even the whiskers on his chin sought permission before they grew.

Everything about him seemed to scream *don't touch*, and surely there was something wrong with Ilaria that her fingers itched to do just that. Test out the sharpness of that chiseled jaw, or if his hair had any of the soft give of mere humans.

Because surely he was something *unearthly. Unreal.*

She should *want* to spit on his shoes, treason be damned, but she could not stop staring. She could reach out and touch a *prince* if she wanted to. The world had been flipped on its axis.

Prince Frediano nodded to the man with the giant, ancient Bible. "You may begin," he said.

His voice was like a terrible strike of thunder, vibrating deep within her, making something completely unknown pulse with heat, rendering her mute. She was rather used to being in charge in her village, though she always gave her elders the appropriate respect. She did not understand this *muteness* she couldn't seem to control.

The priest began speaking in a slow, monotone voice.

Talking about the sanctity of marriage and the sacredness of vows.

The noise Ilaria made when the priest directed the "Do you take this woman to be your wife?" question to the Prince could only be characterized as a squeak. Her head whipped from the priest back to the Prince. She opened her mouth to say something—anything—but only another squeak emerged.

And the Prince said *yes* with shocking ease, as if this made any sense. As if he would have married any woman who'd stumbled inside the cathedral at this particular time.

The priest started speaking again. Ilaria was shaking now, knowing she needed her vocal cords to work but something like terror held her resolutely speechless.

Until the priest looked at her, as if it was her turn to answer.

She still couldn't speak, but apparently she could laugh. Slightly hysterically. Because not one moment of this made sense. Some odd...prank. A clear, *wrong* mix-up. It was supposed to be a dinner. A proposal.

Not a *wedding*.

"I'm sorry" she managed, though the words came out as a croak. "There's been a mistake."

For the first time, the Prince's gaze turned to her. His dark brown eyes—so dark they were nearly black—met hers with such cold, frigid disdain she couldn't form words. But her body trembled—inside and out. She could not fathom *why*.

"There is no *mistake*," he said firmly. "I do not *tolerate* mistakes."

Well, that was suitably terrifying. But she could hardly just *agree* to marry him when he must think she was Sophia. When he was a *prince*, the grandson of the man who'd vaulted her uncle to new heights when he should have been thrown in prison. When, *honestly*, this had to be some kind of hallucination. "I'm not—"

"You are here, are you not?"

"Yes, but—"

"There. She has said yes." His gaze moved back to the priest. "Proceed, Padre."

"No! I didn't say yes to the vow. I'm not—"

But the priest did in fact go on. Why wouldn't he? A prince had told him to. The man with all the power in the room.

"This has to be a dream," Iliana muttered. *A nightmare.*

"I assume you mean that all your dreams have come true. You are most welcome." He even gave a little bow, though she got the impression that impatience simmered beneath every move. "Now the formalities are finished. Let us proceed to the palace." His gaze raked over her. "We'll need to do some work prior to the public introduction tomorrow."

"Work…" She didn't know what that might mean. What *any* of this could mean.

The Prince strode down the aisle. No doubt expecting her to follow. She scurried after him, practically tripping in the borrowed shoes. Sophia's shoes.

She just needed to find the words to explain. To fix this. She could. When the men had come to tell her grandfather of her father's death, *she* had handled

Grandfather's emotional collapse. *She* had suggested he take in the orphans to help at the farm. *She* had handled the rapacious men at the door trying to buy their farm for a pittance.

She knew how to handle tragedies. Surely she could handle this blunder. *For Sophia.* "Wait," she called after him.

He did not wait or even acknowledge she'd spoken. When he came to a side door of the cathedral, he held it open and finally looked back at her.

His dark gaze studied her with such intensity she didn't know how he carried the weight of it. She wanted to stoop, hunch in on herself.

She swallowed and forced words out of her tight throat. "I'm very confused. I don't understand what just happened."

"I would have thought it quite self-explanatory."

"Well, a wedding." She laughed a little breathlessly. Honestly, how wasn't *he* laughing? This was beyond absurd. Then again, looking up at his cold expression it was hard to imagine him laughing *ever*. Did royal mouths even curve that way? She'd only seen dour portraits of him and his grandfather. Suitably proper and royal, but with no hint of mirth.

He pointed out the door. "After you, Princess."

Princess. She was going to start laughing again, and this time she might not stop until she was crying. Or screaming. "There has been a mistake," she said firmly. The same way she'd spoken when she'd told Sophia she would take care of everything.

You've certainly taken care of things, Ilaria.

"Even if you don't like them, there has been one," she said before he could stop her. "Sophia told me she was meant to have dinner with a duke or a lord. I was only going to go through with the dinner, refuse the impending proposal, then go home to Accogliente and—"

"Silence."

Ilaria immediately clamped her lips together. It was as natural as breathing, following his sharp order.

"What exactly are you saying?" the Prince demanded, his voice vibrating with something Ilaria couldn't name, because he clearly kept the emotions behind them locked deep within. But there was *some* emotion there. And it wasn't good.

Still, she had to muster all her courage and set this to rights. Her heart pounded, and her hands shook even as she clutched them together. But she held his dark, intimidating gaze. "My name isn't Sophia. Sophia is my cousin. You've married the wrong woman."

Frediano did not respond immediately. He had learned to temper *all* his baser urges—whether they be anger or greed or lust—by taking his time. He had spent the better portion of his life learning control at the feet of his grandfather, the man who had ruled Vantonella honorably and justly for forty years. The man who had given him safety and purpose and had saved him—literally and figuratively—from the careless neglect of his impetuous parents.

And now that prodigious man's heart was giving out. Doctor after doctor had told King Carlo that if he did not step down from the throne, have the recommended surgery, avoid stress, and *rest*, he would not live to see his next birthday.

Frediano intended to make sure that the great King Carlo lived to see at least twenty more such celebrations. Which was why he had set out to find himself a wife, knowing very well his grandfather would never consider retiring until Frediano was married to an appropriate, sensible woman who would not upset the order of things.

No matter how his grandfather trusted Frediano, Carlo would never risk what had happened before. Not when it came to his only remaining heir. So Frediano had sought the perfect wife. Not a story, not the selfish, press-seeking disaster Frediano's mother had been.

Frediano kept his entire body still as he collected the information this…creature had just laid at his feet.

He had not married Sophia Avida—whose father was a wealthy merchant and the crown's Ministry of Energy, neither titled nor poor, and thus as uninteresting and biddable as any potential princess could hope to be in his eyes—but instead her…cousin.

He had only met Sophia briefly because this union was not about attachment or feeling. It was about being master of the situation he found himself in. It was about convincing his grandfather it was time to step down.

So he'd had a wedding with no guests, and no forewarning to the public. Nothing that spoke of his parents' outrageous, attention-seeking behaviors. He'd chosen a bride who would be pliable, bland, and of no real interest to anyone, so that his grandfather could be certain there would be no embarrassments of the kind his father had heaped on King Carlo's shoulders.

But this woman... "I am supposed to believe that despite looking exactly like Sophia, you are not she?"

The woman clasped her hands so tightly together her knuckles went white, but she held his gaze and did not wither at his accusatory tone.

"I wouldn't say we look *exactly* alike."

Enough alike, if this were true, for him not to tell the difference. Of course, the lighting in the cathedral had been suitably dim and shadowed, all in a nod to keep the public and press from stumbling on that which he would announce tomorrow.

He studied this woman who still stood inside the door, the glow of a sconce highlighting her features. She had the same dark hair as Sophia. Green eyes with flecks of blue. Taking stock, he noticed this woman had freckles dusting her nose and he doubted the sophisticated Sophia spent much time in the sun. Her dress was modest, but expensive. Though a bit ill-fitting around the shoulders.

Borrowed. No doubt from the traitorous cousin. Who'd *known* she was meant to marry a prince this evening. And had instead sent her look-alike *cousin*.

"You are from Accogliente?"

"Yes," she said.

A tiny mountain village of little consequence, far to the north. Sophia had been raised in Roletto, and though not from a royal family, had obtained an education in both scholarly pursuits and in etiquette. Her father was desperate for a title association. Frediano had considered that an asset—something to hold over the man and keep him and his family in check.

This woman from Accogliente would know nothing of how to handle herself in Roletto. She had all the trappings of being an embarrassment. Or a story. Worse, both.

This was a mistake. One he could not afford. Sophia had been the perfect candidate. She was nothing like his mother. She was quiet, pretty and wholly uninteresting. She would not draw attention. She would do as she was told and not be the source of mortification his mother had been. She would not abandon...

Well, that was neither here nor there.

He could demand silence from the padre and the soldier, even from his staff who had the next steps ready at the palace. He could track down Sophia. Demand she marry him. This could be fixed.

But it would take time, and allow for the possibility of too many leaks, too many complications. And the longer it took, the more his grandfather's health stood to suffer.

Frediano had promised his grandfather a perfect bride with a public announcement *tomorrow*, and he would not go back on this promise. He could not return to the palace empty-handed. In the end, he did not care *whom* he married as long as the end result was what he wanted.

Frediano struggled to rein in his temper. To keep the lid on all that seethed and bubbled within him. Someone had thwarted his plan. Had put their own needs ahead of everyone else's. It reminded him too much of a childhood often spent fending for himself while his parents courted the press and performed their outrageous stunts. All their self-absorption had made them perfect for each other. Their "love" for each other had caused wreckage for everyone in their path.

But he was no longer a child, frozen and alone at the base of a mountain his parents had tumbled to their deaths from. No, he was an adult. A prince. A future king.

He eyed his unknown wife.

She would be as boring and biddable as her cousin, he decided then and there. Surely, if she'd had skeletons in her closet, the detailed investigation into Sophia would have brought those to light.

This girl could learn manners. She could learn how to handle herself. He had, once. Perhaps it was better this way. She was new, unmolded clay.

He would turn this *mistake* into a triumph.

It was what he did best.

He, once more, pointed out the door. "We will proceed."

"Proceed?" the woman repeated, her eyes widening and her hands dropping to her sides.

"We are married. You are now Princess... What is your name?"

She blinked down at his hand when he took her by the elbow and led her into the cool evening. She stuttered over her name as he walked her quickly to the unassuming sedan he used when he wished to travel unnoticed. "I-Ilaria Russo."

"Princess Ilaria Montellero. We will go to the palace

and prepare for tomorrow's wedding announcement. You have much to learn before then."

The driver had the back door open as Frediano pulled the stuttering Ilaria toward the vehicle. But she jerked her arm out of his grasp and turned, stubbornly refusing to get in the car.

"The priest said *Sophia*, not Ilaria," she said, holding his gaze, her fingers curling into fists as if she meant to fight him off.

He might have laughed if time wasn't of the essence.

"You only tricked me into saying yes," she continued, keeping those fists wisely at her sides. "We don't know each other. I have a home and people who depend on me and absolutely no desire to become a *princess*."

"The priest will correct any name mistakes *he* made. Knowledge is not necessary for marriage. As for your home, if there are mementos you'd like, I'll send someone for them at once." He did not address the no-desire-to-become-a-princess part.

Honestly, everyone was so against becoming a princess these days.

"I have a farm. I have responsibilities."

"You may sell them." He considered this *more* than fair, if it would expedite this process.

"I don't *want* to sell them. People depend on that farm." Her eyes flashed with temper, which stirred his own.

He squashed the feeling, encased it in ice as she continued.

"You cannot sweep in because you're a prince and take everything away from me."

"I think you'll find that's exactly what I can do."

"This is *madness*." Color had risen on her cheeks, and her green eyes seemed to change with her moods. Perhaps she was right, she didn't look *exactly* like her cousin. She might be a bit prettier—when she was angry.

But Frediano could risk neither anger nor beauty. Only control of the situation mattered.

"I was protecting my cousin from a proposal she did not want and feared she could not refuse. I'm sorry you somehow misunderstood and got caught up in this, but—"

"I do not *misunderstand*. I think you do. Your cousin was not expecting a *proposal* this evening, Ilaria. She knew she was meant to *marry* me. Here. She has deceived me, and *you*."

The woman's mouth dropped open. But it wasn't just shock. There was denial in her eyes. She did not believe him.

Frediano did not need her to, but she had given him a glimpse into the tools he could use to mold her to his will. If she cared for Sophia, fancied herself the protector, she would continue to act toward that goal.

"Her deceit will be avenged, I assure you, but what has transpired cannot be changed. You are my bride, my princess. *That* is final."

"And if I refuse?" she demanded, eyes flashing, those fists tighter now.

Frediano's gut tightened, an unwelcome heat at war with the ice. But the ice would always win. "I could always track down your cousin, if you prefer. Bring her to the palace, willing or not. Make her my princess instead. Because I assure you, *tesoro*, I am not going back to the palace without a wife."

CHAPTER TWO

ILARIA SWALLOWED AGAINST the terror in her throat. Against the betrayal she couldn't help but feel. She did not want to believe the Prince. There was no way Sophia would have used her in such a way.

But, she remembered, Sophia had acted in an odd manner at the train station. Ilaria had chalked it up to fear over defying Giovanni, and excitement over marrying her love.

Now she wondered if it was guilt.

But this was all secondary, because in saving Sophia she had somehow made a terrible mess of things for herself. She could not be married to Prince Frediano. The grandson of a king she loathed. The priest had said *Sophia* while reading the marriage vows, and Ilaria had not truly said *yes*. They were *not* married.

Inexplicably, the Prince seemed to want them to be. Which she knew meant neither legality nor her own wishes mattered.

"What choice do you prefer?" the Prince asked, silky smooth. It should poke at her temper, it should offend her, but his voice caused some physical reaction that was none of those spiky feelings. She did not understand how a voice could make her insides feel warm, make her heart beat so heavily against her chest.

She wanted to run, but she had a *choice* to make.

Neither was a real option, but one would protect Sophia. Perhaps Sophia had knowingly thrown Ilaria to the wolves, but she must have had her reasons. Or maybe she still needed saving. Yes, that was most certainly it. Ilaria could not give up now. She had to be strong. And smart. She would not fail her cousin after promising to help.

Ilaria knew that kings and princes did not care for anyone else's wants or needs. She might have been able to ward off grasping businessmen who wanted her land and government officials who'd wanted to send those poor children off to Roletto orphanages, but she did not know how to convince a *prince* he was wrong.

She could feel the strain of Frediano's patience. Her only *choice*, in this moment, was to go along with this for the time being. Once she was certain Sophia was far enough out of the city, legally married to her sailor, then Ilaria would figure out her own escape.

So, chin held high, Ilaria moved into the car. Though it was dark inside, and smaller than anything she'd expect for a prince, it was still nicer than anything she'd ever *seen*, let alone been in.

The entire inside of the car seemed to warm when the Prince slid in next to her, like he himself was a heater. Though she could not see him as anything more than a shadow, it was as though she could *feel* his gaze, like fingers along her skin.

She suppressed a shudder. She was not well versed in the ways of men and women, but she knew what it meant when a man and woman married.

Surely he wouldn't expect… Well, it did not matter what he expected. *That* was a bridge she would not cross. Even to save Sophia.

"So, tell me, Ilaria Russo," the Prince said, drawing her name out like it was a morsel to be savored. "Would you have come to protect your cousin if you had known a wedding was at the end of the aisle?"

Ilaria didn't have an answer, and she hated that he posed the question. Even reeling, even hurt, Ilaria wasn't sure she would have refused her cousin if she'd known. She'd always wanted to protect Sophia, hurt Giovanni. She likely would have charged in thinking she could handle the situation.

Would you have been able to?

At the end of the day, it did not matter, because Sophia had not told her the truth.

Ilaria looked at the shadow that was a prince and doubted herself, something she did not care for at all. So she turned away, instead watching the lights and buildings get farther and farther apart as the car wound its way up a hill. She tried to come up with a plan. A response. Anything that would keep her *and* Sophia out of this man's clutches.

When the car pulled up to a tall, winding stone wall, she thought perhaps the driver had gotten lost. Or maybe the great stone wall would simply *open* for them, because a prince wanted it to.

Her mouth dropped open as it did just that. The wall

moved, creating an opening large enough for the car to drive through, and then there it was. Even in the dark night she knew the looming shadows and flickering lights were the palace.

She was going to the palace. She had never even *dreamed* of going inside the palace. The only dream she'd ever had about this symbol of royalty was picketing outside the thick stone walls.

"As the days move forward…" Prince Frediano said, his voice a sardonic blade in the dark shadows of the car. Sharp and cutting, yet it did not feel like pain when he spoke. It was a caress, deep inside of her. "…you'll be given many lessons in how to comport yourself, but may I offer lesson number one here and now. Gaping like a hooked fish is *not* how a princess should behave. Ever."

There was that word again. It was baffling enough to accept she was speaking to Prince Frediano Montellero, that she was in a *car* with the *heir* to the Vantonella throne. That his voice seemed to dance along her skin like fingers. But the cherry on top of all that nonsense was the fact he kept calling her a *princess.*

She tried to study him, to convince herself he was perpetrating some bizarre ruse, but the back of the car was dark and he was only an intimidating shadow of a man. She fought off a shiver—of foreboding, surely. "You cannot honestly want *me* to be the Princess of Vantonella."

"Why not?"

"I am no one. I'm surprised Sophia was even an option, but at least her father is wealthy." *If the devil incarnate.* "I'm an orphan farm girl from Accogliente.

I was raised by my grandfather in a little cabin on a very small sheep farm. I know next to nothing about... anything. Except caring for a home and raising sheep."

"You needn't remind me," he returned. Disapprovingly.

His little jab, no matter how she agreed or had pointed it out herself—made her voice sharper than was likely wise when talking to a prince. "No. This is simply impossible. Turn the car around. Take me to the train station. I promise you, it's best for the both of us. We are not married, and we will not be. Beginning and end of this strange little story."

Silence stretched out between them, seeming to throb with portent. When he spoke, though, the words were calm and slow. But unyielding, definitely.

"You seem to be under the impression that my mind can be changed, when I assure you it cannot. I will return to the palace with a bride. It will be you, unless you'd like it to be your cousin."

The way he said it—so final, so cold—it was like a prison sentence. Panic didn't just beat dully under all her other conflicting emotions now, it pounded hard against her chest. She struggled to breathe, to think straight.

She couldn't let him interrupt Sophia's chance at freedom and happiness. But she did not wish to sacrifice her own. She contemplated the only possibility: escape.

Even if it meant jumping out of the moving car.

She reached for the car door handle before she fully thought the action through. She would...jump out. Escape. She would. She *had* to. Surely it was an option no more ridiculous than the situation she found herself in? And if he was chasing after her, he couldn't chase after Sophia.

But he trapped her hands with his before she could complete the movement. Was he that fast? Had she hesitated? She was afraid she didn't know *anything* in this moment, when she'd always prided herself on being ready for *any* moment.

His hands were very, very large. Warm. All-encompassing. This time when her heart thundered in her ears, it felt less like panic and more like something…deeper within. Something she dared not examine too carefully.

"Would you like to tell me where Sophia is?"

"No," she returned, vehemently.

"I could, of course, have her found. In a matter of minutes, my people would be able to drag her back—"

"No!"

He shrugged. She could feel it, as he still had her hands trapped. "Then I'm afraid you are the bride I shall present before my grandfather and our people tomorrow."

Ilaria inhaled sharply. She had to get a hold of herself lest she make an irrevocable mistake. This was a disaster, yes, but not a tragedy. Losing her parents and her grandfather had been *tragedy*. This was simply…a mistake. She had made a mistake. A few, maybe.

She took a deep breath. She needed to regroup. No panic, no attempts at jumping out of cars. She would not get through to the Prince with words or foolish attempts at escape. He had made up his mind—for reasons she would never be able to understand.

Like Mother Nature, he was incomprehensible, unpredictable. She would have to handle him as any good farmer handled the fickle weather. Biding her time, riding out the storm, then cleaning up the mess. But never surrendering to the storm. Never letting it make her give up, no matter how painful the results.

Him holding her hands in his felt like some kind of storm.

"Your hands are rough," he said, as if the fact of the matter surprised him. Or offended him.

She hadn't been expecting poetry, but she didn't particularly expect to be insulted, either. She tried to snatch them away, but he held firm.

"Of course they are," she shot back, trying for firm and disgusted over alarmed and out of her depth. Revolted instead of stirred. She'd pretend he was a boy from the village who'd tried to get his hands on her sheep…and other things. She had no problems rejecting those boys with a stern look and a few sharp words.

The problem was, they were boys. Not even men, let alone princes. And nothing they'd ever said or insinuated had come close to making her feel as though she'd melted from within.

"I've *labored*, which I'm sure is more than you can say." It did not come out strong or scathing. It came out with a shake. "I know how your family views *labor*."

He made a noise, neither confirmation nor denial. Just as though he accepted she'd said words.

The sheer audacity of this man—because he was a man, she had to remind herself. Princes were just men.

Human. With so *many* failings. Though at this point she wouldn't be surprised if he turned into a literal dragon right in front of her eyes.

She tried to picture that, rather than react to the way he still held her hands, like they were stress stones. His fingers moved patterns over her palm, then the backs of her hand. She tried to breathe normally, but there were hitches every time his fingers moved. She tried to pretend her entire body hadn't been engulfed by something she had never experienced before. But she was very afraid she'd read about.

You will not be attracted to this man. He is your enemy.

It seemed no matter what she told herself, her body had other ideas. Completely other reactions. His thumb brushed across the inside of her wrist. She jolted, heat slamming into her body as though she'd been struck by lightning.

She could not see him, but somehow she knew his mouth curved in dark amusement.

Still, she could not manage any stinging words of rejection. No, she seemed to lean forward as though she were magnetized to him, helpless to the sensations his fingers brought out. His hand smoothed up, over her wrist and to her bare forearm.

Her breath caught, though it shouldn't. He was not touching her out of any kind of interest or gentleness. Perhaps he was testing what she was willing to do, and surely she was willing to do *nothing*.

"Let me impart another lesson, Ilaria." He was closer

now, and the way he sounded out her name with his cultured voice had goose bumps breaking out down her arms. He smoothed them away, from elbow to wrist, then back again. "The world is cruel and does not care. Whether you tend your sheep or marry princes. None of it matters in the grand scheme of things. But I am inevitable, and what I deem necessary is inexorable. You can fight me, if you must, but I will not bend."

He let her go, somewhat abruptly. He even managed to create some new distance between them, even though the car was small and the back seat gave him no quarter to move away. Her hands fell to her lap and she suddenly felt…cold. Slapped at. Which jabbed at her temper once more.

"Do you know what they say about things that will not bend?" she shot back.

"Commoners break. I, on the other hand, am a prince. A future king. *I* get what I want, no breaking required."

Ilaria thought that sounded an awful lot like tempting fate, but princes no doubt controlled fate, too. They controlled *everything*.

Not me, she vowed. Somehow, someway, she would get out of this. With Sophia happily married to her sailor. Her uncle incapable of extorting a title. And Ilaria back with her sheep.

She simply had to weather the storm.

The car came to a stop and when he spoke, that deep dark voice sliding around her in the dark, she wondered if that was precisely true.

"Welcome home, Princess."

* * *

Frediano did not often find himself puzzled. Oh, there were a great many problems and challenges in his life, both from being *a* prince, and being the Prince that he was. But these were a bit like war. One developed a strategy, a master plan. One twisted the world to suit the outcome one wanted.

He did not know how to twist Ilaria to what he wanted. The threats against her cousin would keep her obedient for a period of time, but it would not last forever. He would need more leverage.

If she could be the simple mountain village girl, that would be workable. Not ideal, but he'd worked *not ideal* into exactly what he wanted over and over again.

It was her loyalty that puzzled him, maybe even startled him. Her cousin had clearly lied to her, used her, and not considered the lifelong consequences for Ilaria.

And still the woman would trade her future for her cousin's.

Frediano didn't understand it. No more than he understood his fascination with the way Ilaria's hands were rough, her wrists soft. She had flashes of temper, but it was hidden under a softness that made the blade of it all the sharper. Her eyes were intelligent, working through the problem quietly.

A trait he recognized.

He could have dealt with all that, too, and easily. He was not to be outdone by anyone simply because they knew the power of patience and silence.

It was the way she reacted when he touched her that truly concerned him. As if simply holding her hand in his had been a naked grappling in the dark. She was *responsive*, and he found his own needs stirred far beyond his comfort level. She was *nothing* he should find himself having an intense reaction to.

He had chosen Sophia Avida because she was simple. Bland. She would have been the kind of princess no one cared too deeply about, nor sought to make stories out of. He would have been immune to the hitches in her breath, surely.

Or, maybe this odd attraction might have snuck up on him with her as well, if she had appeared. After all, the two women looked disarmingly alike.

In the end, it did not matter if it was Sophia or Ilaria. He would not lose himself in another person as his father often had. A slave to his wife's whims and desires nearly as recklessly as he was to his own. Both at the cost of all else.

The crown. The country. King Carlo's health.

Frediano would never risk anything that might hurt his holy trinity.

So he would mold his wife into what the situation required. Maybe it would be a more difficult task than he'd originally planned, but he was equal to it. And if all went well, his grandfather would step down within the week. Because time was running out.

Frediano emerged from the car, then waited for Ilaria to follow. Attraction would make the act of producing heirs pleasant, he supposed, but that was not the express purpose of heirs. Nor his goal.

His goal was all the respectability his parents had tried to destroy with their reckless choices and disdain for the rules and traditions that had allowed them that recklessness. All they had done had been direct causes of his grandfather's current health problems, even as his grandfather had bent over backward in an attempt to give them all they wanted. Until their actions had almost been the death of Frediano at the base of that mountain, all those years ago.

Ilaria was simply different than what he was used to, and once he trained his body to acclimate to different, he would once again control all his baser urges with his usual aplomb.

"Not getting out of the car does not change the inevitability of the situation," he offered when he had waited far longer than was appropriate for a prince to wait for anything.

He expected her to be contrary and delay even longer, but instead she appeared. She looked up at the palace much like she'd looked up at him when she'd reached the end of the aisle.

The jolt he'd felt then should have been his first clue that all was not right, but he'd been determined to see his plan through.

"It's beautiful," she said, and he knew she was not speaking *to* him, simply speaking. As she was a poor farm girl from Accogliente she had likely never been to Roletto. Never seen the grandeur of the palace that had been built centuries ago for the first King of Vantonella.

Though it was dark, lights shone from inside and out, illuminating the stone walls and dark red shutters, the turrets and spires reaching up for the starry night sky above them like the mountains they were tucked into on the west side. When the sun rose in the east, it would shine on Laga di Cornio, glittering brilliantly and beautifully.

It was a small country, of little interest to the outside world, but proud. Important to him and the name Montellero. He looked at the woman who was his wife in the shadow of the symbol of all he was.

She would not be an embarrassment. He simply would not allow it.

"Follow me, Princess."

"I wish you'd stop calling me that." But she did follow as he strode forward. They would go in the side entrance in the courtyard where he could take her to one of the rooms in his wings with minimal staff interference.

"I'm afraid you'll have to get used to your new title." He had a feeling she had more complaints or refusals on the tip of her tongue, but they reached the door—his aide already holding it open for them.

"Thank you, Eduardo. Is her room ready?"

"Yes, Your Highness."

"Excellent. Have her staff arrived?"

"Yes, sir. Would you like me to show the lady to her room?"

"No, I'll handle it from here. Please tell my grandfather that I have returned and all is as it should be. I'd like to take one last look at the approved press releases before we send them out in the morning." Because while few people knew what had occurred, and what would, there was a plan in place. Secret wedding this evening. Already written and bought announcements that would run in the paper tomorrow, and then the public introduction in the afternoon, as was tradition.

He just had to change the name of his princess before it was sent to print.

"Of course." With a short bow, Eduardo melted into the shadows. Ilaria clearly didn't notice. She was too busy looking around the grand hall. Lancet windows lined every wall, sconces glowed tastefully, but as it was evening and the hall wasn't in use, shadows crowded the corners.

She looked up at the ceiling, where it twisted in a beautiful painting of the sky, into the point of the spire one could see from outside. "It's simply amazing. Someone with very little technological or mechanical help built this place hundreds of years ago, with just ingenuity and their own bare hands, and made it so grand and beautiful that for centuries people have stood under here and looked up. And it has become an enduring symbol of the country. Of your family."

She had concisely put into words what he had always felt. About this room. About his country. His legacy. His role as a symbol. It felt dangerous.

Then she met his gaze, and any awe in her expression died. "No doubt you've never stopped to appreciate the *commoners* who would have actually done the work to build this."

He chose to ignore this comment as he had no plans to *prove* himself to her. "You are now part of that symbol, Ilaria."

Her eyes narrowed, but when she spoke, her voice

was controlled. "I suppose it's a waste of breath to tell you I don't want to be."

"You are correct."

She sighed, looked away once more. "I'm tired."

"I will show you to your rooms. You may rest and then tomorrow you will begin your lessons."

"I can't possibly learn how to be a princess, no matter how many lessons you give me." But she followed as he strode through the hall and then to the entrance to his wing of the palace.

"I learned how to be a prince."

"You were born a prince," she returned.

When he glanced at her, she was taking in every last corbel and painting. Even if she did not love the term "Princess", she was clearly keen on the palace. Or perhaps the *commoners* who'd built it. "Ah, you have not kept up with the royal news, *tesoro*. Perhaps I was younger than you are when I learned, but I was not raised in the palace walls for those first few years. I was a captive of my parents' whims until their untimely demise."

Her silence in response was...odd. It made the words he spoke seem to land uncomfortably, as if she could read all the darkness behind them. The nights as a small child, hungry and alone while his parents were at some party, when they could have simply left him to his grandfather and the royal staff. But no, they had wanted to pretend to be above the throne, above its trappings.

And *he* had suffered.

Which was nothing he should be thinking about when he had his new bride to install in her rooms, press releases to change, and information to uncover about Ilaria Russo.

He would bind her to him in every way, so that she could not get out of this. He would find her every weakness. Because *he* was in control of everything these days. The marriage would be perfect—in his grandfather's eyes, in the people's eyes. There would be no disgrace of divorce, no hint of scandal. There would only be his princess, his future queen, and their serene—if faked—devotion to one another. So that his grandfather could step down and take care of himself.

Frediano walked faster down the halls, but she kept up easily enough. "I don't even remember my mother," she said, as if musing parentage. "She died having me, and my father was killed at Estraz."

Estraz had been a mining disaster over a decade ago. Something like twenty men from a cluster of small villages in the north—including hers—had been killed. It had been a national tragedy everyone in Vantonella was aware of.

Another angle to her story he did not care for. She was more pauper than he liked—the press would focus on this angle mercilessly. So he would have to use every last tool at his disposal to make sure the media did not try to make a story out of her. It would require a delicate balance. So much of this would. But he was, of course, equal to the task. He would make sure of it.

He reached the cluster of rooms that she would inhabit. As his princess. As his wife. Even though he'd been planning on it, albeit with another woman, the reality of installing someone here was disorienting.

He had been alone in this wing since the day of his eighteenth birthday. His grandfather did not come down here, and Frediano was not one to have staff continually about, so he had gotten used to the quiet.

She would upset it.

No. He wouldn't allow that. She would simply do what she was told. She would soon realize that was the best course of action.

He opened the thick door that would lead into her sitting room. He said nothing, walking through to the next door that opened up to her bedroom. He took a few steps inside to encourage her to do the same.

She looked around, not with the same awe she'd had in the great hall, but with a trepidation he did not fully understand. It was a finely appointed room, designed to make any woman happy. Surely finer than anything *she'd* ever seen?

But Ilaria did not look happy. She blinked a few times, then turned a guarded, green gaze on him. She put extra distance between them.

"This is...*my* room?" she asked, and if the hesitation did not give away her thoughts, the way her cheeks flushed an attractive pink would have.

He found himself darkly amused at the nature of her concerns. "Were you expecting something grander?" he asked, endeavoring to make his expression surprised.

"Don't be ridiculous," she returned, her eyebrows drawing together.

"Then what is your concern?" he asked silkily, moving closer to her, the small distance between them seeming to warm and dance with possibility.

She *was* his wife after all. He had been looking for a wife who was nothing out of the ordinary. She mostly fit the bill. So much of her was average, her height, her build in the ill-fitting dress, even the rather dull brown shade of her thick, wavy hair.

But her green eyes, their ever-changing shades and hues, were intriguing. Alluring. If she used them as weapons, they could in fact create chaos.

He would have to be certain she did not.

"I don't have a concern," she managed, though her voice came out strangled and her cheeks grew pinker, her breathing quicker.

Deep within him, he felt the chains of his control pull. He wanted his hands on the flush of her skin. Wanted to see if it covered the rest of her body. Would there be other rough parts of her like her hands, or would she be soft all over?

"I suppose in your village husband and wife share a room," he offered, taking another step so that they were nearly toe to toe. So that he could examine those eyes, that flush, and test her.

She stood, rooted to the spot, looking up at him. He did not know if it was courage or fear that kept her from retreating. It did not matter. Both could serve.

"I—"

"And a bed," he added, as if it had only just occurred to him. When quite frankly a bed had entered the equation when she had jolted under his touch. When she had leaned forward in the car, not away.

She should not intrigue him. This was not the plan— and he never made plans he did not stick to wholly—but here he was. With an altered plan, with an impossible attraction to the wife he had not chosen.

But he would not give in.

Perhaps she would, though.

She shook her head again. "I wouldn't—"

"We, of course, will." That too, was inevitable. And much like her eyes, all too alluring.

She made that same noise she'd made back at the cathedral. A kind of inelegant squeak. But she did not turn away. Did not *run* away. She held his gaze, as if trapped there. The woman *did* have a backbone.

Even if his was stronger.

"You are my wife, Ilaria."

She shuddered out a breath, and he could not speak for the surprising and disarming bolt of need that shot through him. The heat, the violent claws of it. He wanted her naked beneath him, in that big frivolous bed.

Now.

But that would not do.

He would control this lust. He could. If he enjoyed bedding her, so be it. She no doubt would enjoy the same.

But he would not be ruled by his traitorous wants that led to ruin. So he eased himself back. To the door. To somewhere he could get a handle on his control. There was time yet for the duty of making heirs, and he would make sure it was appropriate.

"But you need your rest tonight. Tomorrow you will be introduced to our people," he said through gritted teeth. "Sleep well, Princess." And with that, he left her.

And cursed himself for being a fool.

CHAPTER THREE

ILARIA HAD NOT settled for some time after the Prince left her. She was battered by feelings she did not want—all physical, all beyond her control.

She'd never felt that way before. At home, she had too many responsibilities to worry about things like *attraction*. She had long considered marriage out of the question. She had too many people depending on her to worry about finding love and partnership, and she had assumed attraction and chemistry were by-products of such.

Clearly, she had been very wrong. And it was hardly the only thing she'd been wrong about.

Sophia had *known* what fate she was condemning Ilaria to. Ilaria wished she could believe the Prince a liar, but unfortunately there was no logical explanation except his.

And still, Ilaria chose to stay. To protect her cousin. If she ran, Frediano would no doubt go after Sophia *and* her. If she stayed…

It was so unfathomable. How could she be married to a *prince*? The symbol of everything she blamed her father's death on. The grandson of the man who had no sense of her loss, of her people. Who believed Uncle Giovanni's cost-cutting measures and dangerous greed made him the perfect choice for Minister of Energy.

She could not become *part* of everything she loathed. Her father and grandfather would certainly roll over in their graves.

But how could she condemn Sophia to that fate when her cousin had someone who loved her, wanted to marry her, and get her away from her terrible father and a life she hated? If Ilaria ran, how would softhearted Sophia stand up to a prince when she hadn't even been able to stand up to her father?

Ilaria thought of the dark, foreboding Frediano. The way he made a woman, even one as strong as herself, feel. Not weak, never that, but unsteady. As if he willed earthquakes wherever he walked.

She sank onto the bed. It was like lowering herself into a cloud, and nothing like her rough sheets at home on her small, lumpy bed.

There had to be a way out of this without endangering Sophia's happiness. If Ilaria had to be married to a prince for a time, *she* could stand up for herself. Would. And somewhere along the way she would figure out how to extricate herself from everything she loathed.

She would just have to ride out this storm.

She flopped back onto the bed, looking up at the ceiling. It was a beautiful mural of angels floating above the mountains and a large alpine lake. Gorgeous. Everything about the palace was absolutely stunning.

And so very much not her home.

Exhaustion deep in her bones, she crawled under the silken covers, pulled off the uncomfortable borrowed dress, and fell into a surprisingly restful sleep.

She woke with a start to *people* in her room—marching around while sunlight streamed in from floor-to-ceiling windows, offering a stunning view of Lago di Cornio sparkling in the sunrise.

"Are you ready for breakfast, Your Highness?" A woman asked from a respectable distance away.

Ilaria's stomach growled as she pulled the sheets up to her collarbone. She hadn't eaten since the train, but she did not know how to proceed.

"Aurora, fetch the robe," the woman said without waiting for Ilaria's answer.

Aurora, presumably, walked over to a large wardrobe, opened it and Ilaria gaped at all the clothes inside. Then she remembered what Frediano had said about gaping fish last night and closed her mouth.

"I am Noemi, your personal assistant. If you need anything, you simply ask me and I will make certain it's done. Today, we have a very tight schedule."

Ilaria was handed a robe. She felt there was no choice but to pull it on. Much like the sheets it was one of the softest materials she'd ever felt. Reasonably she understood a palace and a prince would have the best of the best things, it was just she'd never even been able to *imagine* the best things.

"The Prince has sent up a breakfast for you in the sitting room." Noemi gestured at the door. Clearly a sign that Ilaria was to get up and stick to the schedule.

"I... I need to make some phone calls. There are people I need to speak to."

Noemi hesitated a moment, something flickering in her gaze and then disappearing before Ilaria could parse it. She nodded. "Of course. Why don't you come get settled in for breakfast? I will see about...obtaining you a phone."

Ilaria would have preferred to go to a phone right now, but she didn't feel comfortable ordering this woman around. Personal assistant or not, Ilaria was not accustomed to people waiting on her.

"Maybe you could just show me to a phone and—"

"Come. Eat," Noemi interrupted smoothly, gesturing Ilaria toward the door. "You'll want to keep your strength up today."

Ilaria got out of the tall bed as gracefully as she could manage. She followed Noemi into the sitting room. There were pretty, comfortable-looking chairs arranged around a coffee table filled with trays full of more food than could feed her, or even the two new people in this room.

Her stomach rumbled, but she did not sit. "This is... far too much. Far too elaborate." It could feed her entire village.

But Noemi chuckled. "Nothing is too elaborate for a princess on the day of her royal introduction."

Royal introduction. Ilaria desperately needed that phone. Needed to make sure Sophia was safely married. Safely hidden away somewhere.

Then she'd get out of this place. Dig an escape tunnel out if she had to. Swim across Lago di Cornio. *Anything.*

"I'm not sure I can eat until I can make a phone call and check on things at home."

"If you sit and eat, I'll go fetch a phone for you. If I'm not back by the time you're done, Chessa here will begin the fitting." Noemi gestured at one of the two women in the room. They flitted around a rack of gowns, a platform and a full-length, three-paned mirror that faced it.

Ilaria wanted to argue. Or run screaming, but she had promised herself to ride the storm. So she swallowed down her objections and took a plate and put some food on it.

Noemi smiled. "I will go track down a phone for you." Then she left the room.

The seamstress studied Ilaria with speculative eyes. Ilaria was not used to such attention. She managed a smile and took a bite of a soft cornetto filled with chocolate cream so good she worried it might ruin her for all other food.

"These are beautiful," Ilaria said, gesturing to the gowns, attempting to make conversation. "What are they for?"

Chessa and the younger woman, maybe an assistant or apprentice, exchanged strange looks.

"Surely the Prince…" Chessa trailed off, then smiled brightly as if that could erase the words. "An announcement of your marriage to the Prince will be made, and you will appear before the people of Vantonella as an introduction. You will need a gown, of course."

Right. That.

"So we must get the dress ready. Quickly."

"And then Noemi will help you prepare your speech," the assistant added helpfully.

But Ilaria felt the cornetto turn to ash in her mouth. "Speech?" she repeated. She was sure she paled as well. Frediano had mentioned an announcement, an introduction. But not speeches.

Chessa waved this away, as if it was simply of no consequence when she was expected to stand up in front of *all* of Vantonella and *speak*. "Not so much a speech as a few words. Mostly waving. And the kiss, of course."

"The...kiss."

"For the official marriage photograph printed in the papers."

Ilaria looked from Chessa to the assistant and tried not to feel as though they were speaking a foreign language.

Official marriage photograph. Pictures and speeches would make it much harder to escape this. It would make her known, complicating any escape once she knew Sophia was safe. Complicating everything, because everyone in the *country* would know.

That she'd married a prince. That she had stepped into the world she had spent most of her life railing against.

She desperately needed that phone. "When does all of this happen?" Ilaria asked, hoping she sounded casually curious and not hysterical.

"Three this afternoon, Your Highness."

That did not give her much time to convince the Prince she was unsuitable, while also convincing him

Sophia was beyond his reach. There had to be some third option. A compromise.

"I must insist you finish your breakfast," Chessa said. "I'll need time to accomplish alterations, and the Prince will have my head if I do not."

"The Prince should worry about himself," Ilaria grumbled, then winced, because obviously this woman was *employed* by the Prince, and loyal to him. Not her.

"The Prince worries about everyone, Your Highness."

Ilaria felt suitably chagrined, though it was ludicrous. Why should she feel shame for speaking poorly of the man who'd all but kidnapped her? Quite frankly she deserved a few angry words. And an *escape*.

She definitely had to escape before there was any kind of speech.

Or kiss.

She shivered—the bad kind, surely, because though the Prince was handsome, he was her captor, and she did not *want* to kiss him. Truly.

She'd never kissed *anyone*, and now she was meant to kiss a prince? In public?

"Let us begin." Chessa pointed to the platform.

A dress was simple. Certainly not irrevocable. And Noemi would be back with a phone she could use soon. And then she could speak to Sophia…

What? What then?

She'd figure something out. So she stepped up onto the platform, and then had to fight discomfort as the assistant pulled the robe off her. As the two women commented on her body and slid a dress off the hanger and then helped her into it.

When Noemi returned, she was empty-handed. But she smiled brightly, likely at Ilaria's obvious dismay. "A phone is on its way, Your Highness."

From behind Ilaria, Chessa spread out the skirts of the fine dress. "These colors aren't right at all. Not with her coloring."

"I'm afraid the Prince was very clear that these were the types of dresses he preferred," Noemi returned.

The seamstress muttered a string of rebuttals, then spent the next half hour putting Ilaria into and out of dresses. The gowns themselves were no hardship to wear. Each was more beautiful than the last. And so surprisingly comfortable. The beige ones stayed on the rack and Noemi's frown deepened with each jewel-toned addition Chessa offered.

Just as the tension in Ilaria's stomach doubled with every minute a phone did not appear.

The last gown was made of dazzling beading that glittered like jewels. It was stunning. Like nothing Ilaria could have ever imagined. Yet it hugged every curve and dipped dangerously low so that she held her hands over her chest while the seamstress tugged and pinned and muttered to herself.

"This is the one," Chessa said without hesitation. "The others are far too plain."

"The Prince requested a beige dress," Noemi cut in. Repeating herself.

Clearly, Chessa did not fear the Prince. "Nonsense!

He'll want his princess a glittering jewel. Men know nothing of fashion. We shall alter the beaded gown."

Spitefully, Ilaria wanted to agree with Chessa. If the Prince would hate it, this was the dress. But she was deeply uncomfortable with the cut. "Isn't it…" Ilaria trailed off as three sets of eyes looked at her, as if surprised to find her a breathing human being and not a lifeless doll. "It's rather revealing, isn't it?"

Noemi smiled kindly. "You look beautiful in all of them. However, the Prince—"

Before Noemi could finish the sentence, the door to the sitting room opened—no knock, no hesitation. Because princes likely never knocked or waited to be given permission to do anything.

Frediano opened his mouth but did not immediately say whatever greeting he'd been planning on. He paused. Ilaria felt his gaze move over her, like a flame being held to every inch of her previously cold skin. He had looked at her like this last night. Like he might devour her whole. Like, inexplicably, she might be attractive to a *prince*.

Which she surely did not want, no matter how her body reacted.

Then the heat went out of his eyes, just like last night. Cold. A switch that could be turned off. She should be happy that he could and would.

But she found herself yearning for things she did not fully understand instead.

"This is not the correct dress," he said.

"No, Your Highness, but it suits her much better," Chessa replied, chin held high.

The Prince looked at the seamstress with such frigid disdain that Ilaria nearly wilted *for* her, but the woman simply held his gaze.

"I did not request one that *suits* her. I requested the one I required." He turned to Noemi, effectively cutting off the seamstress. "You will correct this error immediately."

"Yes, Your Highness." Noemi curtsied quite gracefully, and immediately disappeared with the seamstress, her helper and the beige dress.

Leaving Ilaria behind in the sequins, and far too much skin showing.

"I have requested a phone," she said so she'd stop thinking about the dress. And the way he looked at her with heat in his eyes. "I need to make some phone calls."

Frediano looked around the room, not responding. There were two people cleaning up the breakfast trays. "Leave us," he ordered with a flick of the wrist.

They scattered. No, that wasn't fair. Scattered suggested something *she* would do, or sheep might. The staff *melted* away as if they'd never been there in the first place.

Then, he pulled a mobile out of his pocket. He even smiled as he held it out to her.

She did not trust that smile. When she reached out, it was gingerly, but before she could take the phone, he continued.

"I'm sure you will want to speak with Sophia, but you needn't bother. I have already done that for you this morning."

For a moment, Ilaria felt as though her knees might

give out. But she stiffened them. She could not stiffen her arm. It fell to her side.

"It turns out that, strangely enough, she did not make it across the border with her…sailor last night." Frediano frowned and shook his head, as if it was too bad. "She and Tino were, shall we say, very kindly detained."

Ilaria wished she could have absorbed this information as casually as he delivered it, but her breath caught with a stab of pain. Because she understood what he was telling her. What he was doing.

It was a threat. No, it was *blackmail*.

"Now, as the Prince, I could let them go, of course. Across the border, to marry and live whatever lives they've planned."

"Yes, you could," Ilaria managed, trying to keep her voice caustic instead of despairing. She was quite certain she failed. "Why did you bother with a wife when what you want is a prisoner?" she demanded, impotent anger coursing through her.

"You are not a prisoner," he replied with a laconic shrug.

"You're blackmailing me!"

"No, *tesoro*. You have a choice. You just don't like the choices."

He was arguing semantics, so there was no point continuing the verbal argument. He was right in a way. Two options. Hurt her cousin or hurt herself. Give her uncle what he wanted by handing Sophia over to the Prince, or lose everything that mattered to her, when she'd already lost so much.

Frediano had effectively trapped her. Into gowns and speeches and kisses for royal portraits.

They faced off in silence, Frediano with a small, satisfied curved to his mouth. Ilaria doing her best not to hurl her fists at his chest. It would do nothing, and no doubt she'd be thrown in a dungeon or something equally archaic.

And Sophia would not escape her father. Uncle Giovanni would get what he wanted.

No, it could not happen.

"But to show you how generous I am, I am prepared to offer you a gift of sorts."

She snorted, which was probably not the mark of a princess, either. All the more reason to indulge. "I find that very hard to believe."

"Believe in me always, Princess. As it only took a quick glimpse into your life to understand that jewels and furs and castles would not be the way to your heart."

"*Hearts* have nothing to do with this," she returned acidly.

"Indeed they do not. At least, mine does not. Yours does a little, according to your neighbors."

She felt thrown thoroughly off axis. "My…neighbors."

"They told my men many things about you. All glowing, of course. Excellent for a future queen. But mostly they spoke of your devotion to your under-the-radar and potentially illegal orphanage."

This time, her knees just didn't weaken, her vision blurred. He would threaten her home? The people in her care who had lost so much already? She had to stay strong. She had to fight. "It isn't an orphanage," she said, trying to remain cool.

"A work home?" he suggested, feigning an innocence he'd likely *never* had.

"It is *home*," she returned, and had to curl her hands into fists over the low dip of her dress.

"A home for some, perhaps, but there are four under-age children, with no parents, living on this property. Neither you nor any of the other adults are the legal guardian of any of them, correct?"

"I knew your grandfather was a thoughtless fool, but you are a soulless—"

The calm, self-satisfied expression with which he'd been delivering his information fell off his face in a flash. He stepped closer. "You will never, ever insult my grandfather, your king, again," he said, so quickly, with that same frigid tone he'd used on the seamstress. But there was fury in his eyes—heat, not ice. He took a few moments to cool it. She watched it happen, fascinated against her will.

When he spoke again, he was calm. "Not *everything* is a threat. As I said, this is a *gift*. Insurance, if you will. I will not shut down your little organization. I will instead lend it some legitimacy."

"I don't need—"

"Upon the completion of the marriage announcement this afternoon, a trust will be set up to fund not just your operation, but an expansion of your farm in Accogliente. For every year you do not cause a scandal in our marriage, an increasingly large amount of money will be placed in this trust. When you supply me with an heir, the trust will be moved into your name and theirs and be completely under your control. You can help your village, your orphans, whatever you wish, however you wish."

Ilaria was shaking. She tried to control it, but this was some sort of...devil's offer. It was so much of what she wanted.

And it would bind her to him. Forever.

"How do you know that's what I want?" she managed to ask.

"My men are very thorough, Ilaria. And your little orphans are very forthcoming when people ask the right questions. You should probably teach them a better distrust of strangers."

A violent wave of reaction went through her. That he would use everything she loved against her. So quickly. So easily. Because *this* was what royalty was. Cruel and selfish and only interested in their own incomprehensible whims.

"I hate you," she seethed.

"Do you?" Frediano returned, unbothered and unsurprised. "When I am making you such a generous offer? That doesn't make much sense."

It was generous, maybe, but certainly not selfless. At best, it was a payoff. At worst, it was another layer of blackmail.

One that would help so many. Help the village. It would help *everyone*.

Except her.

She closed her eyes against a wave of grief.

"You may thank me."

Ilaria opened her eyes, meeting her *husband's* cold gaze and vowed to herself that *someday*, she would find a way to get revenge on him. *Someday* he would wish he'd never said *yes* in that cathedral.

But when his dark, impenetrable eyes settled on her dress, thoughts of revenge scattered. She wanted to back away. Run away. But she was held still by the sheer force of his gaze.

"Drop your hands," he ordered.

Some part of her felt compelled to obey immediately, but the thought of him seeing so *much* of her… She shook her head, cheeks flaming with heat.

"I'm afraid I must insist."

"You're not afraid of anything." Was he? Surely even a prince feared something?

"Would you like me to drop them for you?" He said it silkily. Like it was a promise, not a yet another threat in what felt like an avalanche of them.

But she found her hands dropping nonetheless. It was his voice. Perhaps there was some sort of drugging quality to it. It reverberated inside of her until she lost herself, when she could not afford to lose herself.

"You are surprisingly beautiful, Princess."

"I…" She had never considered herself *beautiful*. Her life had not been about how she looked, ever. It had been about what she could do. For her grandfather. For her farm and the children. For Sophia.

His gaze was on her eyes—but she could not help the feeling that he took her *all* in. Over and over again. The more her pulse beat, the more she did not wish to cover herself any longer. She felt like her whole body was becoming a pulse of something. A good something. An exciting something.

Her body seemed determined to betray everything she was.

"Now that we have successfully determined what *appropriate* dress you will wear," Frediano continued, "we will go over what will be required of you to say. And do."

"Do," she repeated.

He smiled then, not mirth or blackmail, but something...wicked. "Indeed, Princess. I will introduce you to our people. You will read Noemi's carefully prepared speech. Only a few lines. And then we will share a kiss."

She was not sure how he could say the word and make her feel like he had touched her. When she had never once been kissed before. Had never had time to think about wanting to be kissed.

"It is a tradition going back centuries—paintings and then photographs. Only my parents have broken this tradition. I do not intend to follow in their footsteps. In anything."

That he said seriously. As seriously as any vow.

This was all so overwhelming, and what made it so much worse was *him*. The way he looked in his dark suit. The way his gaze made her feel like she was ablaze. The way her mind kept going back to the thought of *kissing him*.

Kiss this man. As if she were his wife. His princess. A future queen.

When she only wanted quiet and her farm and the old

life where she was the one helping people and wanted nothing for herself.

But there was a want inside of her now she was afraid to name. It grew with every moment they were alone. With every moment he regarded her and did not look away.

She could not go back in time. She could only go forward with what tools she had. She had learned that after her father's death, and it had served her well. It had turned her into a strong woman who figured out how to handle the challenges life threw her way.

If she did as the Prince said, Sophia would be safe, her people back home protected, maybe even elevated. And if she was miserable in the process... Well, she would rise to that challenge. Find a way to turn this strange and awful turn of events, this misery, into a positive.

Ride out the storm. Somehow, she would.

Frediano could all but *see* her thinking, pulling herself together and readying herself for the war ahead. Admirable, but she would need much more of a poker face if she was going to survive being royalty.

So she would, because he had found the key to keeping her under his thumb. He had been surprised to learn of her little farm/orphanage operation. It was impressive, he could admit, what she had done with so little. And how well liked she was in her village, according to his men's reports. Her kingdom was tiny, but loyal. He could appreciate that on its own merit, philosophically.

But this was reality, not philosophy, and in reality,

her reaction to him spoke volumes. She was horrified by the lengths he was willing to go to ensure her obedience, but she was not horrified by the heat between them.

He knew better than to play with fire, but surely he could handle a little spark? "Which part concerns you so, Princess? The speech?" He stepped closer. "Or the kiss?"

She held his gaze, chin jutted stubbornly. He was tempted to smile, though her challenge should frustrate not amuse.

"I have no concerns, Your Highness," she said, and then she smiled. Or tried. The bitterness in *Your Highness* was a little too clear to believe smiles. "Perhaps you should tell me yours."

He laughed. If only such a challenge fit into his life, but all that mattered was molding her into the perfect princess that would convince his grandfather to step down and focus on his health.

She frowned at his laugh, and then deeper when he put his finger under her chin and raised her face so she met his gaze.

"We are adversaries, *tesoro*. I will not be *confiding in you*. Ever. This is a marriage, and it is a battle. I intend to win." No one's wants would threaten his grandfather's health, most especially his own. He would control this as he had controlled everything for so long.

She struggled with something. Her innate need to challenge him, no doubt. But she did not immediately argue. Did not childishly state her intent to win instead.

She sucked in a deep breath, which brought his gaze down to the low dip of her dress.

Yes, she was quite beautiful, and it would not do for anyone to know just how much. The beige dress, the boring newspaper article. Any spark of how interesting she truly was hidden so no whiffs of similarity between her and his mother were made. King Carlo had to think her wholly different.

"I think it only fair we try to reach a compromise." She tried to smile again. It did not reach her eyes. "I can give a small speech, but we could abstain from any kissing as there are no romantic feelings between us and never will be."

He slid his thumb across her jaw, almost without thinking about it. Like his fingers had a mind of their own. But her skin was so soft. "This is not a negotiation. It is tradition." He smiled at her then, wanting, perversely, not her sad attempts at compromise, but her challenge. "Don't tell me you're afraid."

She jerked her chin from his fingers. And his smile widened.

"Perhaps the real concern, Ilaria, is that hidden away in your little village, taking care of other people's children, you have never, in fact, kissed anyone privately let alone publicly." She sucked in such a breath he knew he was right. The reports on her had unearthed no suitable men in her life, but one never knew exactly what was done behind closed doors.

She made it clear *nothing* had been done.

"Do you worry you will bungle it?" he continued. "Or do you think perhaps a kiss from a prince might be so different you are afraid of swooning in front of our people?"

Her struggle was valiant, to not let her surprise or irritation with his words show. But she failed.

"There is that gaping I warned you about."

Her eyebrows furrowed again, anger causing those green eyes to turn a stormy gray. Fascinating, really. Perhaps she was some kind of mountain witch.

But she did not speak any more. No vehement *I hate you*. She was silent. He had given her two very strong reasons to hold herself back. He had twisted *her* world to make sure it *had* to suit his.

As *kings* did.

"Perhaps you are worried that you will jolt at my touch, as you did last night." He'd relived the simple pleasure of dragging his thumb against the soft, velvety expanse of her wrist, over and over in his bed last night.

His body tightened—the dreams he'd had of possessing all of her on that ridiculously frivolous bed in her bedroom were too close to the surface. *Playing with fire will always get you burned*, his grandfather had warned him often as an adolescent.

So he had learned. You could not *control* fire, but you could learn to *endure* anything. So he had.

His control was his armor. It was who he *was* and how he survived. And in this *battle*, it would see him winning yet again.

"I worry about none of these things, *Your Highness*," she said, managing to make the honorific sound like some kind of insult. Her voice was cool, composed.

Impressive.

Everything about Ilaria Russo was turning out to be surprisingly impressive.

The way she seemed to glisten like the sea in this sparkling dress. The ill-fitting fabric from last night had not accounted for the way her body curved. He had trouble trying to not imagine his hands gripping the flare of her hips, her rough hands on him—

She was a *temptation*, but he reminded himself he liked proving his control, time and time again.

He stepped back from her, offered her a cool, polite smile. He put the mobile on the table next to a breakfast tray. "The phone is yours, Princess. Feel free to contact whomever you wish. Once the introduction is made this afternoon, I will instruct my men to let your cousin go. Should you need anything, you need only ask Noemi."

He gave her a little bow, smiled at her with just enough princely courtesy to have her frowning outright.

And then he left to prepare to introduce his princess to his people.

CHAPTER FOUR

ILARIA WAS POKED, prodded, moved about and basically treated like one of her sheep. She was not a woman with her own thoughts or opinions. She was *livestock*.

And there was nothing she could do about it as long as the Prince held her cousin captive.

Three o'clock loomed closer and closer. Women came in and out of her rooms to prepare her.

She was dressed in a gown nothing like the jeweled one from this morning. It was beige and, though clearly elegant and expensive, plain. Her hair was done in a similarly simple manner. An army of people lathered and painted at her face and somehow made it look... different. Not glamourous or like a princess, but more like a slightly shinier, less freckled version of herself.

She looked at herself in the mirror and did not know how to feel. On the one hand, no one would find her interesting if she looked like *this*. Except to question perhaps why the Prince had chosen her. And she did not wish for anyone's attention, so it seemed...right.

But part of her wondered why she couldn't at least *look* like a princess, even if she did not wish to be one.

"Are you certain about this?" she heard one of the makeup people ask Noemi.

Ilaria met Noemi's gaze in the mirror. The woman's slight frown immediately turned into a reassuring smile.

"This is exactly what the Prince requested," Noemi said brightly. Which was not an assurance that she looked particularly beautiful, only that she met the Prince's requirements.

"Maybe the Prince shouldn't always get what he requests," Ilaria muttered, causing the young woman straightening the *beige* collar of her gown to giggle.

Noemi began to gather up all the staff, giving them soft orders. Ilaria found she couldn't think of anything to do but sit here and stare at herself in the mirror.

She was reminded too keenly of that first day after her father had died. How she'd been lost, powerless to stop a relentless chain of events.

And then you pulled yourself together and figured it out.

She had to find some kind of faith that she could do the same in the midst of this unfathomable string of events.

She had called Sophia four times on the mobile Frediano had given her. Each time she had left a message. Sophia had not returned any calls. Ilaria couldn't help but think that if Sophia would at least call her back, she might find that faith.

"Is there anything I can do to help you feel any more prepared?" Noemi asked.

Ilaria looked up at the woman—her *assistant*—and blinked at the tears that threatened. She was stronger than tears. "You've been wonderful." Ilaria did her best to smile at Noemi. But she was sure it failed because there was *nothing* to smile about. "Thank you for all your help."

"It is only my duty." Noemi looked at the piece of paper Ilaria hadn't touched since Noemi had handed it to her. "Perhaps you'd like to practice your speech?"

Ilaria hadn't even been able to bring herself to look at the words. Almost as if seeing them would make this real.

It's real all right.

She lifted the paper. *Good afternoon, citizens of Vantonella. I am so happy to be here this afternoon. Thank you for your most kind welcome into the family Montellero.*

She closed her eyes against the words and resisted the urge to crumple the paper. She was *not* a Montellero. She was a Russo. Her grandfather and father had been proud of their family name, and with the orphans and farm under her care, Ilaria had never given any thought to changing that. Marriage had always seemed a luxury meant for other people with fewer responsibilities and more time.

But this was not a real marriage. It was a rescue mission. It had been her father who had always told her she must look out for Sophia. That while it might seem her cousin had all the things Ilaria did not, the Avida home was not a warm or loving one. And it would make her mother proud if Ilaria did all she could to forge a relationship with her cousin and protect her in whatever small ways she could.

So maybe this was a disaster, but at the very least she was making her parents proud.

Ilaria swallowed the lump in her throat. The pain she felt was not new. It was an old loss. Grief that never fully went away.

"It is time for us to meet the Prince, Your Highness."

"I don't suppose you'd point me to the nearest exit and not sic the guards on me when I run?"

Noemi's eyes went wide in alarm. "I'm sure that won't be necessary."

Ilaria had to laugh at the woman's discomfort. "I'm sorry," she said, putting a hand on the woman's forearm. "It was a joke."

Noemi smiled tightly. "Of course." She clearly did not find it in the least bit funny.

"Follow me."

Ilaria was led through the maze of hallways that made up the palace. In order to calm her nerves and keep her mind busy, she began to make a to-do list. One would be to get a map of the palace so she could memorize it.

Or figure out the best exits anyway.

She was ushered back into the gigantic room she'd first entered last night, with its gleaming windows and amazingly impressive ceiling, built centuries ago.

For all the ways she did not want to be here, for all the ways this was a nightmare come to life, this room simply *awed* her.

And very much against her will, so did the man standing in the middle of it. She hated him. Truly and totally.

But he was so very handsome. He stood next to another man, whom she would have recognized—even at this distance, and even if he wasn't the King of her country—as Frediano's relation. They shared broad shoulders, dark hair—though the King's was sprinkled with gray—and an unsmiling mouth that could easily be called cruel.

Holding themselves in the exact same manner, ramrod straight and hands clasped behind their backs, they studied her approach as if she were a lifeless piece of art.

She wished she was.

She glanced back once, to find that Noemi had disappeared. Melted away like all the palace staff seemed to. It left Ilaria feeling adrift. Abandoned.

But there was no choice, at present, except to move forward. To stand before the King and Prince and somehow behave as if this was *normal*.

Frediano inclined his head in a kind of bow as greeting, though there was no deference in the gesture. "Grandfather, I would like to introduce you to my wife. Ilaria, this is my grandfather. Your king."

He is not my king. Ilaria knew she was meant to curtsy. Even a country girl who'd never had any dream of meeting the monarchy knew this was the sign of respect required.

But she didn't want to, couldn't seem to force her knees to bend. She stood, silent and still, working so very hard not to do the one thing she so desired: spit on the King's shoes. For her father. For Accogliente and Estraz.

"Ilaria." There was warning in Frediano's tone, but

she could not seem to heed it. This man had *promoted* her uncle. Rewarded him for all the ways he'd put his own wallet over the hardworking men in her village.

"She is shy, Grandfather," Frediano said, with some humor she doubted he felt. "And not accustomed to the ways of the monarchy just yet. But I will ensure she has all the proper training."

"Excellent," King Carlo returned, nodding. His voice was as deep as his grandson's, with a hint of gravel. But that was not what Ilaria couldn't help but notice or study. Frediano spoke differently to his grandfather. Not just deferentially as required by title, but almost with…true warmth. There was a softness in his dark eyes when he smiled at the man who'd all but sentenced her father to death.

"Do you have a voice, girl?" the King asked her, but he did not sound angry. Not even impatient. There was no inflection whatsoever.

But him calling her *girl* certainly had her emoting. "Yes, Your Majesty," Ilaria replied, telling herself to bite her tongue, and losing the battle. "And, as I'm twenty-four, I'm hardly a girl. Which is good news for your grandson as I'm not sure a child bride would suit the image you're trying to curate."

The King's eyebrows rose, but he did not offer any kind of scolding. Of course Frediano's frigid gaze warned her she'd likely get one from him later.

She inclined her chin. Frediano had said she could not create a scandal if she wanted to ensure her cousin and farm were taken care of. He had *not* said holding her tongue was a condition of the deal.

It's blackmail, not a deal.
And she'd do well to remember it.

Frediano prided himself on being able to read people
quickly and accurately. His one and only challenge these
days was his grandfather, who had keeping things close
to the vest down to an art form.

Frediano hoped that in the years to come he could
find his grandfather's level of detachment, but perhaps
there was simply too much of his mother in him. Perhaps he could not completely hide his emotions, but he
could control them. So he did not reprimand Ilaria or
ask her what the hell she thought she was doing talking to the King in such a manner.

He took her arm instead and followed his grandfather down the hall at enough of a distance that Carlo
would not overhear their hushed conversation. "You
look lovely this afternoon, my wife," he offered, smiling pleasantly.

She offered him the same smile, though her eyes
flashed. "No need for dishonest flattery, Your Highness." She looked at his grandfather's back, then up at
him. "My cousin is not returning my calls."

"I assure you it is no fault of *mine*," Frediano replied. "Perhaps she is too embarrassed or guilty to take
your call."

Ilaria's dark eyebrows drew together, as though she
wanted to argue with him but could not find the words
to do so.

"You must let her go," she said instead.

"And I will. The moment we are done with your introduction." He smiled down at her. "You have my word."

"Your word means *nothing* to me."

Frediano's temper flared, but he had been watching his grandfather too long to let his emotions show. He kept his arm relaxed, his expression bland, and any of the rage he felt was allowed to burn and bubble deep inside, but only there.

They walked side by side down the long hall. At the end were the double doors to the terrace, flanked on either side by staff who would open it for them at the appropriate time.

Outside, the King's aides would be setting everything up and would signal when it was time to make their entrance.

King Carlo turned his dark gaze to Ilaria. He surveyed her, but Frediano could not hope to gauge what his grandfather saw. Hopefully, the kind of quiet, obedient princess that would allow him to feel comfortable in stepping down.

Not the woman so *disgusted* by the idea of him giving his word.

"You have been apprised of what is expected of you today, I hope?" the King asked Ilaria.

"Yes," Ilaria replied. Through gritted teeth.

There was a long stretch of silence where both Frediano and his grandfather waited. And waited. And waited.

Frediano had to give himself a moment before he spoke to make sure his tone came out measured. "When speaking to your king, Ilaria, it is customary to use 'sir' or 'Your Majesty'. To curtsy when you first approach and when you leave."

Ilaria remained stubbornly silent, making eye contact with neither of them. She looked straight ahead at the doors.

"She will need that etiquette training as soon as possible," King Carlo muttered.

Torn between frustration and boiling fury, Frediano forced his mouth to curve ever so slightly at his grandfather. "Yes, sir. I wholeheartedly agree. No need to worry for this afternoon, though. Noemi has prepared her thoroughly. Hasn't she, Ilaria?"

For a moment, those stormy green eyes met his. "Of course. *Sir.*"

This time the heat boiling in his gut had very little to do with anger, but both responses were dangerous, so he looked forward. At the ornately carved door and shining gold knob. She wished to be challenging. Unfortunate, but not impossible.

Nothing was impossible.

"They are ready, Your Majesty," one of the doormen said, bowing at King Carlo.

The King lifted a hand. "Go ahead."

Each man pulled open a door. King Carlo moved first, out onto the ornate royal terrace that looked down over the large courtyard in the front of the palace. As predicted, hundreds of Roletto citizens stood below, eager to hear their king speak. To catch their first glimpse of the new Princess who had only been announced this morning.

Frediano stepped forward, Ilaria's arm in his. She

took the first few steps easily enough, but as they moved into the sunlight, as the crowd came into view, she stiffened.

She tried to pull her arm from his grasp. She even moved to take a step back, so he held on to her more tightly. "There's no turning back now, Princess," he said into her ear, quiet enough his grandfather wouldn't hear as he used the microphone to greet the crowd.

Ilaria's breaths began to come in pants. He looked down at her, noting the way her eyes darted over the crowd. She was...terrified.

Against his will, he remembered his own first time here. After his parents' death, he had been in no shape to be shown to the public. His grandfather had secretly purchased a remote mountain chalet and taken him there. For three months, he'd given Frediano the space to recover and prepare for his new role—far away from all these eyes.

But eventually, Frediano had needed to face his future. He had been placed on this very stage three months later. Eight, nearly nine. Terrified that so many eyes were on him. He knew, too well, what it was like to step out onto this terrace, being wholly unprepared for an entire capital city interested in *him*.

He had *felt* wholly unprepared, but not as out of his depth as she must be—he'd known he was royalty, even if he'd never known his grandfather prior to his parents' death. He'd been used to paparazzi, to a certain amount of *attention*. He had been given three months to prepare as his body came back from the brink of death.

He'd been terrified, and a child, but he had not walked in totally blind.

Ilaria came from nothing. A small mountain village with fewer people in the entire town than were gathered in the courtyard. She was from a family with no connections—save an uncle by marriage—who, as far as Frediano had been able to surmise, had no connection with the Russos.

Ilaria tried to step back again, but Frediano held her firm. There was no going back now. He remembered what his grandfather had whispered to him all those years ago.

And thanks to those words, and his grandfather's support, he had gotten through it.

So would she.

"Count your breaths, *tesoro*. It will do no good to faint. In, one-two-three. Out, one-two-three."

He was surprised that she listened, breathing carefully and no longer attempting a retreat. Perhaps fear was stamped all over her features, but she breathed. And as she did, she became less rigid.

Oh, she looked like a terrified gladiator about to be thrown into a coliseum full of lions. But she no longer seemed about to run.

She was brave, this mistake he'd made. Strong in the face of the unknown. Unwilling to let her terror win. A strange feeling wound its way through him. Something almost like pride.

When his grandfather turned and signaled for him, Frediano...hesitated. He did not for the life of him understand why, but it felt like a betrayal to drop her arm like he was supposed to.

When the only betrayal would not be accomplishing his duty. Still, when he stepped forward, for the first time in his life, he did not follow tradition—in this case approaching the microphone and the crowd alone before bringing his new bride to his side.

He found he simply could not let Ilaria go when she gripped his arm like it was an anchor.

So, as he stepped forward, he brought Ilaria with him.

CHAPTER FIVE

IT WORKED, SOMEHOW. Counting. Breathing. The crowd was still overwhelming, but Ilaria didn't feel the need to run. She breathed. She counted. She held on to Frediano as he spoke, though she heard nothing of what he said.

He had become her anchor in a sea of panic. She didn't know how or why. Usually she only had herself to grab on to. Her sense of right. A *cause*.

Your cause is Sophia. You make it through this, and she gets a life. Your cause is your farm and the things you could do to help them with all that money he has promised.

Right. That helped, too.

She felt Frediano maneuver her closer to the microphone, and that was when she was finally able to concentrate on the words he was saying.

"I hope you will all warmly welcome your new princess. My wife. Ilaria Montellero."

My wife. Montellero.

The panic returned, doubled, tripled. But she thought of Sophia being free to marry her sailor. She thought of her uncle's face out there somewhere—it would kill him, that she had taken Sophia's place. That he would not get his title. It was revenge. If everything else was terrible, and, *oh, it was*, at least there was that.

She was to hold the paper in a manner so that no one could tell she was reading from the paper, but the arm Frediano held was supposed to be how she did it and… She couldn't let him go. She could not explain it, but she would not have the courage to speak without his stabilizing hand.

Everything felt more like a buzz in her head than any words, but still she thought of what little she'd read. And then she thought of what she'd want to hear if she was…them. A citizen of Vantonella. A citizen of this country and this monarchy.

She looked out at the sea of faces. It was too overwhelming, so she fixed her eyes on the great Monte Morte in the distance. Its peak was white with snow, the rest dazzling, craggy grays. The sky so blue she had to squint.

"Hello." That wasn't right. What had the paper said? "Good afternoon, citizens of Vantonella." Her voice shook and she knew she had to get it under control. She was an expert in faking bravery when she had none. "I am…" Not happy. At all. If she said she was happy she might burst into hysterical laughter. "I am honored to be here today." It wasn't the right word, either, but at least it didn't make her laugh.

Even as she held on to the strong, warm arm of the Prince, she reminded herself she had *some* kind of power as a princess. Surely she could do something to make these people feel like they might be…important.

Heard. She kept her eyes on Monte Morte, and as she spoke to the crowd, her voice got stronger.

"I hope that I can offer a new voice to the monarchy. One connected to those of you who work for a living. Who have suffered great tragedy. I hope I can speak for all of you, in my way, and offer you a voice here among those too far removed to understand." She dared a look at Frediano, at King Carlo. Neither betrayed a response. She wondered if she'd ever be able to build that kind of formidable stoicism.

She held Frediano's gaze as she said the rest to the people. "But I understand. I will always understand. Thank you."

Frediano's granite expression gave nothing away as she stepped back from the microphone. But he dropped her arm.

She had no idea why that felt like a loss.

Brief loss, though, as he put his hands on her shoulders then and pulled her forward. His gaze did not change, nothing about him *changed*, but she remembered the part she had been hoping to avoid.

The kiss.

He leaned down, close enough she could feel his breath against her skin. She could feel his warmth... everywhere. In his hands on her shoulders, in the darkness in his gaze. She forgot about the crowd, the King. Everything centered on his dark, fathomless eyes.

She did not want to kiss him. She desperately reminded herself over and over again she did not *want* this. Her body seemed to think otherwise.

Because she did nothing to stop it. She did not move

away from the finger that brushed against the collar of her dress, making her skin prickle with electricity and warmth, making that deep throb inside of her so all-encompassing she could think of nothing else.

His lips touched hers, and yes, just like in the car last night she jolted. It was *electric*, what a simple touch could do. Hands or mouths, it did not matter. Her skin seemed charged with something that only came to life when they touched.

She did not understand it, did not *want* to understand it. But she was helpless to it all the same. His mouth on hers, a gentle brush of contact that seemed to sweep inside her like light and heat. So she only wanted to lean forward and find more.

But his hands on her shoulders tensed, held her there and out of reach. He looked down at her, cold and forbidding.

"I hope you are happy, Princess," he whispered, making her shiver. "You have ruined *everything*."

There was a great cheer, his grandfather waving at the crowd, and then the exit. Frediano thought of it in steps, instead of his reaction.

Out the door. Into the hall. Face King Carlo.

His grandfather's expression betrayed nothing, but Frediano thought his complexion had paled. He could not ask his grandfather if he was feeling all right in front of all these people, but he worried and would have to send a message to his doctor as soon as possible.

"Frediano. We will discuss this in my office. Young

lady, I hope you are better prepared to follow tradition and protocol when we have the royal wedding dinner."

"Royal wedding dinner?" Ilaria blinked. "But we're already married."

King Carlo only sighed. "Frediano."

"I assure you, sir, she will be thoroughly prepared for the dinner. You needn't worry. She will be perfect."

King Carlo looked at Ilaria with a hint of disbelief but said nothing. Just nodded to his hovering aide and then turned and walked away.

Frediano held himself perfectly still. So many different things roared through him. Fury that she'd *dared* to say whatever she wanted—creating a story no doubt the press would eat up like candy. A voice of the people. A princess ready to fight for the common man.

Exactly what he'd been looking to avoid with someone as bland as Sophia Avida.

His grandfather now questioned her suitability, and this would ruin the timeline. It would jeopardize his grandfather's health, and it was too late to go back now. She was his wife, introduced to all of Vantonella. He could not discard her and go demand Sophia marry him. That would be a disgrace as damaging as his parents' scandals.

And if that were not disastrous enough, he'd wanted more than the chaste kiss on that balcony. He'd wanted to kiss her until those misty green eyes were bright with passion. He'd wanted to feel the gentle shiver of her body everywhere. He had *wanted* so much that it had almost overridden everything else.

He had resisted his wants for decades now. They did

not matter. They did not factor. His wants were nothing to the needs of Vantonella. To his ailing grandfather.

Because that was all she was—a *want*. Not a need.

No matter how his body wished to betray him and present her as one.

"Let me escort you to your rooms, Princess," Frediano said, offering his arm.

She gaped at him, but then seemed to remember his warning about doing so and snapped her mouth shut. She looked at all the people around them as if deciding who might help her escape.

But there was no one. She took his arm and walked back to her rooms in complete and utter silence. With every step he felt her tense, more and more until by the time they stepped into her sitting room she was like a wound top ready to explode.

He dismissed everyone, shut the door, and then looked at her there in the boring dress she'd somehow managed to make look beautiful anyway. Made herself interesting with her words *anyway*.

She whirled on him. "I never want to do that again."

He raised a brow. "Which part? The kiss or the part where you went off script and ruined everything?" He congratulated himself on how bored he sounded when what he wanted to do was rage.

She looked up at him, eyes wild, doing enough raging for the both of them. "All of it," she said fiercely, her hands curling into fists as they had last night and again this morning. "I have been introduced as you desired. Let my cousin go and…and…lock me in a dungeon or something. I never, ever want to stand in front

of a crowd that size again. I do not want anything to
do with this dinner, your traditions or your protocols. I
would rather be alone in a…prison. Forever."

He looked down at her, surprised by this reaction.
She had panicked initially, but then she'd spoken quite
beautifully to the crowd. Even if it wasn't what he'd
wanted or could tolerate, the crowd had been rapt. Now
she looked like she was panicking all over again.

"I did not expect theatrics, Ilaria."

She looked up at him, defiant and angry but still with
that edge of desperation he did not care for, because it
made him wish to reach out and calm her.

When she *should* panic. She had caused a mess.

She whirled again, began to pace. "I hate it. I can't
do it ever again. How does anyone stand it?"

"Perhaps there are people out there who crave to
be dissected by all and sundry, but I am not one of
them. Still, I am a Montellero. It is my duty." He looked
down at her, fighting too many urges to name. "You get
used to it." Was that gentleness in his tone? He needed
to harden himself. Make sure she understood that she
could not cross him. Not ever again.

"I am a Russo," she returned, fiercely. She came to
stand in front of him, like she might jab a finger or fist
in his chest. When he raised both eyebrows at her, her
hand fell, but she did not shut up.

"We mine. We herd sheep. We do not *speak* to
crowds. We do not care about protocols and dinners."

But she had certainly worked up a crowd. The papers
would scream about the people's princess, and people

would want to know *all* about her tragedy. Fury rose in him, ruthlessly tamped down.

"You prefer to work in the shadows. Collecting your sheep and your orphans, speaking of your work and your tragedy. You prefer to thwart rules and laws with your *illegal* orphanage. But your preference is no longer material. You are *not* a Russo any longer. You are a Montellero. And you've just crowned yourself the voice of the *people*. That you did all on your own."

"I only wanted to say something…that would comfort me to hear if I were in their shoes. Don't you care about your people at all? Or is it all tradition and protocol?"

"Did it occur to you tradition and protocol is for them as much as us? Did it ever occur to you that this is not all one-sided? We are a symbol. We are leaders. Tradition is *comfort*. It is stability. In a world *full* of tragedy and upset, we offer something to *rely* on, Princess. And now they will rely on you. You wish to disappear, to be thrown in a dungeon. I wish I could arrange it, but instead you've made yourself a point of interest."

"I did not mean…"

Anger was winning. He could feel its claws sinking so deep inside of him he'd never pull them out. He should step away from her. Leave this room. Do damage control.

But he only wanted to step closer. To impress upon her all she'd done. To make it clear to her she was a mistake and he did not tolerate mistakes, even his own.

To put his mouth on hers and devour instead of giving her chaste, public kisses that were only symbols.

"You have compromised everything I set out to do. You have put your king's health in great jeopardy. *You* have failed, and symbol or not, protocol or not, *I* do not accept failure."

"Then I suppose you should end this farce," she shot back.

"There will be no *end, tesoro.*" An annulment would be a scandal perhaps bigger than his parents' flouting of Vantonella tradition. No Montellero royal had ever divorced, and he would die before he became the first. "You will atone for your sins, one way or another, *Princess*. You wish for a dungeon, you wish for your little village… Well, you have permanently ruined any chance of having those things you so desire. But consider this marriage prison enough for us both."

She sucked in a breath, a mix of panic and her own brand of anger that poked at his. "My cousin…"

"Your cousin can go to hell for all I care." It was the absolute wrong thing to do, and Frediano knew better than to follow his impulses, but in the moment it was either storm out or pull her into his arms.

He chose to storm.

He had to get control of himself before he faced his grandfather. He walked to his grandfather's office slowly, counting his breaths and steps—that trick he'd given Ilaria not so long ago.

Today, it did not help. He stood outside his grandfather's ornate office door waiting to be granted entrance, and *boiled*.

How had some little mountain girl ruined him so

completely? Just because of the color of her eyes and the depth of her reaction to him? It was unconscionable.

The door opened, one of the King's aides gesturing Frediano inside. His grandfather sat at his giant desk and waved him forward as well.

"Come. Sit."

Frediano did as he was told, doing everything to contort his face into the same expression his grandfather wore. Stoic blankness.

King Carlo looked down at a stack of papers on his desk. He was not a man who liked computers, so most things were printed out for him. It was one of the few things Frediano planned to change once he was in that chair.

He studied his grandfather's face for signs of strain and was somewhat relieved to find no new ones.

"I have read your reports and spoken to the aides on the ground," King Carlo said. "I instructed the guards at the border to let Sophia Avida go on her way. We have no use for her now."

"Grandfather—"

King Carlo raised his gaze. Brown, blank eyes stared back at Frediano. How many times had he searched those eyes for some kind of reaction? He'd never found it.

"Frediano, I am surprised at how this all turned out, and yet it seems to be quite a success."

The apologies were on the tip of his tongue before the word *success* penetrated. He blinked. "Sir?"

"My advisors tell me we are viewed as too traditional, too masculine. I thought a sweet, feminine girl like Sophia Avida would be good for that, but… I think your choice might suit better. I liked what she had to say. It will soften us, and the people will like that. Her tragedy will provide much sympathy for her, and in turn you. I'm not sure Sophia could have done such for us, even if her father is in my ministry."

"I…fail to understand."

"You've done well, Frediano."

For a man who twisted the world to suit him, he did not expect his grandfather to somehow twist his own failure into a…success.

"She will be of interest, but not a scandal. Nothing like your parents, spoiled and self-centered." His expression darkened for the briefest moment, before returning to blank. "Her background is interesting." Carlo tapped his fingers on some papers Frediano assumed were the report on Ilaria he'd had sent over this morning. "Everything she's done seems to be quite selfless— whereas a pampered girl from a wealthy family could not have been viewed as *that*. Even if your princess is not as selfless as she seems, tragedy softens people's hearts more than a good pedigree. It is a great tool, when used correctly. We shall use it correctly, yes?"

Frediano felt almost as unmoored as he had when he'd first stepped out onto the palace terrace as a child. This was not what he expected. This was not what he'd *planned*. But he knew how to roll with the punches, did he not? "Then you'll consider your doctor's advice?"

"Not yet," King Carlo replied, frowning. "You must teach the girl some protocol. Some…obedience. She is of good clay to mold, but she must be molded before

I feel comfortable stepping down." He fixed Frediano with a steely stare. "The royal wedding dinner must go well."

"So it will," Frediano vowed.

CHAPTER SIX

ILARIA FELT LIKE she was going to break into a million pieces. Her rooms were large and beautiful, and still the walls felt like they were closing in. Hours passed. She was served dinner in her room. She called Sophia so many times she'd stopped leaving messages because the box was full.

She wanted to cry and wail in her bed, pound the pillows a few times. She wanted to run far, far away. Back home where her world made sense and *she* was in charge of it.

But this was not the first time the world had pulled the rug out from under her. It was simply more difficult this time because there was no one to turn her attention *to*. No one to comfort or care for.

It was just her, alone, in this opulent room.

She'd thought to change, but the wardrobe was full of clothes that were just as over-the-top and fine as the one she wore, and she wasn't sure she'd be able to undo the buttons on the back of this dress without help.

She didn't want help. She wanted to get out of here. Even if only for a few moments. A walk outside, fresh air, some reprieve from this prison would calm her. Soothe her.

You wish for a dungeon, you wish for your little village... Well, you have permanently ruined any chance of having those things you so desire.

Those words echoed in her head, in the fierce, furious way Frediano had said them. She supposed it was something. Anger and fury over that icy control, or the utter blankness of his grandfather.

But that didn't truly comfort her, because he was so infuriating, so...arrogant and controlling and *awful*, but he made her feel overpowering *need*. She hated him, and she wanted to touch him. He had *ruined* her life, but he had held her arm and steadied her when she'd wanted to fall apart.

No one had ever given *her* support before. She wished it hadn't been as comforting and steadying as it had been. She shouldn't find comfort from someone ruining her life. Even if he *had* made an effort to help by telling her how to breathe and focus.

Everything he did *for* her was for his own ends. And the powerful attraction between them... She did not know why or how he could make all her thoughts simply vanish. All her wants change into his touch. She had never experienced such a thing.

She was a woman who enjoyed taking care, in helping. She was not a woman who'd ever spent any time considering her own needs or wants.

For a moment, that thought stopped her cold. Was that...wrong?

But of course not. She was a helper. That was a good

thing. Better than being selfish and ruining someone's life simply because they could.

She went to the door that led into the hallway. She paused at it. Noemi had tried to keep Ilaria abreast of all the rules and protocols of moving about the palace, but Ilaria had been too upset to listen. Or maybe she'd simply been in denial.

Now she wasn't quite sure how to proceed. *If you are really stuck being the Princess, you get to proceed however you want.*

She knew that wasn't true, but she decided to hold on to that thought anyway. She pulled the heavy door open and stepped into the hallway.

There was a man right there, dressed in what she was realizing was a kind of palace uniform. Expensive black suits, all perfect and gleaming for the men. The female staff seemed to have more choice in their attire, but it was always black.

"Can I get something for you, Your Highness?"

Never call me that again! She wanted to scream. Instead she smiled at him. She'd decided somewhere along the way to treat them all as she had treated any new orphan or widow when they'd come to the farm in distress.

With them she remained calm. Smiled warmly, and never danced around the subject at hand. So she did the same now. "I'd like to get some air. Outside."

The man gave a slight bow. "Allow me to accompany you, Your Highness."

"That won't be necessary, of course." If there was one thing she *had* done before this afternoon's mess, it was familiarize herself with the palace map.

The man looked a little stricken, but he quickly regained his composure. "I'm afraid I must insist."

Ilaria breathed in through her nose, let the breath slowly out of her mouth. She did not allow her fingers to curl into fists. She smiled at the man. "What is your name?"

"Vincenzo, ma'am."

"Vincenzo, are you my jail warden?"

His whole face fell. "N-no, ma'am. Of course not."

"Then I would like to walk alone."

"I'm sorry, Your Highness, but I simply can't allow it." And he seemed the first in a long line of staff members who apologized to her today that truly meant it. "The paparazzi are everywhere. Your speech caused quite a stir. While the castle is protected, many have found ways of getting glimpses into the outer courtyards where you might walk."

Her speech. Why hadn't she read from that paper? Why had she thought she might grab some control in this situation? Frediano was right. She'd ruined *everything*.

She wanted to collapse right there, throw herself on the ground and have a tantrum. As if he sensed her hovering on the edge, Vincenzo quickly stumbled on.

"But I can show you a private path outside you could use. I simply must insist on going with you, though."

It was something, Ilaria supposed. The cool night air, even with the company of a stranger, was better than staying in that room suffocating. "All right. Thank you, Vincenzo."

When they stepped outside, it was pitch-black save

for the moonlight and a ribbon of dim lights that lined a path out toward the lake and then around.

"See the lights?" Vincenzo asked, pointing down the pathway. "If you truly wish to be alone, you may walk to the end of them and back. I will stand here and watch." He smiled encouragingly, as if he was giving her a great gift.

She supposed in his way he was. So she offered him a smile. "Thank you, Vincenzo."

He bowed and she left him there. She'd find an answer in this walk, just like she did in her walks back home when she was sorting through a difficult problem. She loved nothing better than to hike through the mountains, the sheep, feel the wind whip her face and remind her that her problems in this great, wide world were small indeed.

Each step down the path brought her closer to the lake and its soft, calming lapping sounds. She felt hugged by the dark, calmed by the chill in the air. She could take a deep breath again.

No problem was so big she couldn't solve, she decided. Or perhaps tried to decide. Just because Frediano thought she'd ruined everything didn't make it true. Just because the King called her a girl and insisted she needed more work didn't mean she had to *care*.

She hated the King.

It was strange to have seen him up close. To see a flesh and blood man whose indifference had sentenced her father to death. To have seen Frediano's reaction to him, one of warmth and devotion, with so little of it returned. She wondered if anyone knew what the King thought or felt about *anything*. Did Frediano?

It was as if considering the Prince conjured him from the dark. She heard the sounds of water different from lapping, turned, and there he was. Emerging from the water, the silvery light of the moon outlining his wet, exquisite form.

Surely, she was…hallucinating? But he stepped out of the water and walked toward a bench, where a large towel was neatly folded, alongside a few other things she couldn't make out in the shadowy dark.

He was so handsome. Unfairly so. Like in a a fairy tale, tall and dark. Dangerous and compelling. A wolf. A prince. A *villain*. The water dripped from his hair, from his body, and he moved to dry it.

The Prince. *Your husband.*

She blinked at that truth she was still in denial of. But here she could only stand, stare.

Want.

No, she could not, *would not* want him. No matter how her traitorous body throbbed in protest. Her body's reaction was its own, but her thoughts could be controlled.

She wondered if swimming alone could cut *those* muscles into his body, or did he work out in other ways? It really didn't bear thinking about.

Really.

"You should not be alone," he said by way of greeting.

"I'm not," Ilaria said, cursing herself for the squeak

in her voice. "Vincenzo is watching me." She pointed back to the man closer to the palace.

Frediano looked, then lifted his hand—a wave, a dismissal. Vincenzo bowed and then disappeared into the castle.

So she was alone. In the dark. *With my husband.*

No, she would not think of him as that word. He was the man she hated. Her jailer. Her *kidnapper.*

"What…are you doing?" she found herself asking, even as her brain instructed her to walk away. Back to the palace. Back to *jail.*

He scrubbed the towel through his hair, regarding her in the shadows. "I swim the lake every evening at this time."

He was back to himself. No more biting anger. Just that controlled detachment, so like King Carlo. Ilaria hated that almost as much as she hated him. "I'm quite certain I saw *two* pools on the palace map."

"A swim in the lake is not the same as a swim in the pools. I much prefer the lake, and at night, even the papparazi with their long scope lenses cannot find me."

Ilaria watched, fascinated as he drew the towel down over his chest. "Is it not cold?" she managed to ask, only sounding slightly breathless.

He stopped drying off and met her gaze in the dim light between them. "That is the point," he said, an edge of darkness to his words that matched the darkness around them.

He pulled a sweatshirt over his head and began to walk toward the palace, and she knew he expected her to follow. So she stayed rooted to the spot. After a few more steps he seemed to realize she had not followed. He turned to face her. The lights of the pathway allowed some sense of him—his outline, his features, but something about the dark made her heart jitter in her chest. Like she was in danger.

Of course you're in danger. This mad man has tricked you into marriage. Into giving up your life. Forever.

She had to return her focus to the reasons she was here. "My cousin—"

"Has been granted her freedom," Frediano interrupted. Causing her to gape at him. He'd said Sophia could go to hell. And now...

"My grandfather was quite impressed with you," Frediano continued, shocking her even farther. "He ensured Sophia was granted access to cross the border with her sailor. You needn't worry about her. She has found what you will not."

Ilaria simply didn't know what to do with this information. That King Carlo had been the one to let Sophia go felt...incongruous. To everything.

"*He* thinks you'll be an asset to the crown," Frediano continued.

The emphasis on *he* brought her back to reality. "But you do not."

"I am not King. Yet. It does not matter what I think. In fact, it does not matter at all. You are my wife. That will not change."

Not just a sentence, but a threat. That there would be no end to this marriage—there was too much at stake when every year saw more money and autonomy for her farm and orphans. Even if she could give that up, she couldn't simply disappear home, even with an annulment or divorce. Her life was irrevocably changed. She was *known* now, and she did not know how to accept this any more than she knew how to accept this man as her husband.

"Come, Princess. I will walk you back to your room and safety." He offered his arm.

"There is no safety to be found here."

"More than you'll find with scheming journalists and relentless paparazzi," he returned, sending a dismissive wave to the high walls that protected the castle at night.

Her eyebrows drew together as she studied him. There was something that simmered in the way he said those words. "You really hate the press."

"Yes," he replied simply.

His reasons didn't matter, and yet in that way she was drawn to him on a physical level, there was a part of her desperate to understand this confusing man who'd ruined her life. Her father had always encouraged her to find the best in people. The mining accident had changed that for her and her grandfather, but it was still an ingrained habit.

So she asked the simple question. "Why?"

Frediano had not expected the question. He considered not answering. It was, after all, none of her business. But if he was going to fix the mistakes made in the past twenty-four hours, then he had to learn from them as well.

She was not going to take orders—likely too used to

giving her own in her little fiefdom she'd created. He was going to have to shape her to his will in some other way. All the reports on her that his men had given him insisted Ilaria was a kind, giving woman who worked hard and told the truth. A rational woman who somehow survived despite all the ways the deck had been stacked against her.

Surely that meant she had a quick mind to be rationalized with. Perhaps if she understood, he could find a way to control this situation completely.

"My parents used the press to suit their whims, mostly in a bid to hurt my grandfather over and over again." He walked as he spoke, being careful to recite facts over the dark, swirling feelings. "They lied, and the press ate those lies up. Got rich and fat on the discord between father and son. Fell for every stupid trick in my mother's book of deceits." *And tried to drive my grandfather to an early grave.*

"You disliked your parents very much," she said softly, finally catching up to walk next to him. Though she never took his arm.

He had the strangest urge to reach out and take her hand in his. He ignored it. "They were hardly parents," he said, looking up at the palace. "They kept me from my grandfather, from my birthright, not because they wanted some better life, or simpler life as they claimed, but because it got them more attention than following tradition and protocol could."

He slid her a glance. She didn't bristle like he'd thought she might at the words *tradition* and *protocol*.

Instead, she seemed to consider. When she met his gaze, those green eyes were soft.

"Did it hurt at all when they died?"

Another question he had not expected, but he did not outwardly react. Instead, he considered his answer. He remembered that day, being alone. Of being certain he would follow their fate. For days. Nothing but snow and hunger and certain death.

All because they hadn't wanted to leave him behind since it did not suit their image. Nannies were seen as a sign of detached parenting practiced by the wealthy, and his parents liked the image that they loved him so much they could not bear to part with him. He wished he could assign some sort of love on their choices, but they had always spoken in front of him as if he did not understand what their words meant.

Even when he hadn't, he'd understood what their actions meant. They cared only for themselves, not *him*, and for how they could get others to fawn all over them.

So he had been certain no one would care that he was frozen and alone at the base of a mountain his parents had fallen from.

Until his grandfather had found him, dug him out with his own two hands and saved him. Not just from that mountain, but from that childhood.

"It was a relief," he returned, though that was too simple a word for all the complicated feelings of that time.

"That must have been difficult," she said softly.

He looked down at her, surprised by the softness in

her tone. Moved, more than he wanted to be. "Do you pity me, Princess?"

She jerked her chin up. "Of course not."

"Good."

"I was devastated when my father died. He was my life, my light. And my grandfather's. Our world went dark that day."

"I suppose it did for many in your village."

"You are correct. And do you know why?" She stopped her walking and turned to him. "Because men like your grandfather and my uncle cared more about money than safety. And in the aftermath, when my grandfather was a wreck, and prospectors wanted to buy our farm, and widows and orphans walked through my village like ghosts, *your* grandfather promoted my uncle to his ministry. *Your* hero decided orphans who'd lost everything should be ripped from their homes and sent to the city and their shabby establishments."

Her eyes flashed—not with temper so much as hurt. And though he recoiled against the anger and accusations against his grandfather, what he heard in that diatribe told him many things he could use to mold her into what he wanted.

"And where was *your* grandfather in all this?"

"Mourning," she shot back at him.

"And you, a girl of fourteen, was not?" They stepped into the palace, and the lights were low as it was late. He could hear nothing but the hushed sounds of her harsh, irritated breathing.

"It sounds as though, much like my parents, your grandfather left *you* to the wolves," he continued. To anyone observing them from afar, it would seem husband and wife walking to their rooms. As long as they didn't look closer at the bitter, muttered words. "More destroyed by his grief than grateful for his gifts."

She whirled on him, there in front of her sitting room door. "My grandfather was ten times the man you or your grandfather could ever hope to be. If he had a weakness it was *love*, and that is not a weakness you could ever hope to *imagine* being felled by."

She did not say it, but he felt the words all the same. *If your parents did not love you, who could?*

Love. His grandfather had loved his father, bent over backward to try to keep his son, but all his son had ever done was betray him. His parents had claimed to love each other, but all they'd ever really loved was themselves and the attention they could find from others.

Never him.

All he'd ever seen come from love was *wreckage*.

He could tell she was ready to whirl back around and storm into her rooms, but something possessed him to keep her here. With him. He pressed his palm to the doorframe, blocking her unless she pushed it away or ducked under it.

She did neither. Her shoulders came back. She glared at him. Still in that ridiculous beige dress from this afternoon that did nothing for her and yet he felt a yearning so deep inside him he was convinced she could be dressed in a shroud, and it would not stop this inexorable, impossible *lust*.

But control it, he would.

"I suppose that gives me some insight into you. However, I must warn you. If you ever speak to the press about my grandfather, ever threaten the sanctity of our name, you will *wish* for the dungeon you requested."

"Sanctity," she said, each syllable dripping with disgust. "You wouldn't know the meaning of the word."

He reached out, drew his finger down her cheek, an impulse he would curse himself for later. She shuddered under his touch, even as she glared at him. At least this impossible heat between them was mutual, no matter what *intelligent* feelings they might try to hold on to, chemistry held them in its bonds.

And he found he could not resist poking at it, moth to flame. He leaned closer, so close her eyes widened as their noses were only centimeters apart.

"You hate me, curse me, blame me." He leaned so now their lips were merely a whisper away, giving himself one last moment of torture. "But you want me."

Her breath caught and her cheeks flared a deep, alluring pink. "No," she said, but it was a whisper. More hopeful than truthful. Her breath dancing against his mouth like a promise.

"Would you like me to prove it to you?"

She laughed—or tried, though it came out breathy. "You could never."

"A challenge" he murmured, and in one move she was clearly not expecting, he pulled her to him. He did not wait or hesitate, when he should have until they were somewhere private. But he did not. He simply crushed his mouth to hers.

At last.

He expected her to push him away. To fight. But instead, she melted. She shuddered beneath his hands and leaned into him. Her palms pressed against his abdomen as she moved to her toes to better meet his mouth. His hands moved, though he had not given them permission to travel up her neck, to cup her face, to angle her mouth just so under his.

To take the kiss deeper, darker. To drown in the warmth of her, the innocent openness of the way she kissed him back.

She whimpered against his mouth, her hands smoothing up his chest, and he...detonated.

He had underestimated her. A tactical error that poisoned his blood before he had a chance to correct it. And then there was only the taste of her. Dark and vibrant. Like the shadows of the mountains she came from. His hands streaked down her sides, curling into the fabric, desperate to rid her of this *beige* encumbrance.

He wanted to see where the sun hadn't touched. He wanted to taste every inch of her, this surprising beauty he did not understand.

He wanted...

But that was the problem, and eventually the *want* reminded him of who he was. What he could do.

And what he couldn't.

Rip her dress off in the here and now, where anyone in the palace could walk by and see his loss of control was out of the question, wife or not. A display of passion so out of character, so like his parents, would no doubt get to his grandfather and ruin everything.

Still it was harder than it should have been, to ease his mouth away, to uncurl his fists from her dress. To end the temporary madness that had ruled him, however briefly, and never could again.

She looked up at him, lips swollen, chest rising and falling in a tantalizing seesaw while her eyes were wide and clouded with a lust he wanted to slake here. Now.

Though his blood raged, his body hard and wanting, he stepped back. Away. She was a danger. To everything. And though it was a physical pain to beat back the desperate pulse of desire, pain was simply a reminder that he was doing what was exactly right.

He would have full control over every last urge before he had her in his bed. So that he always knew he could walk away. So that he always knew *he* was in control of everything.

He would take her on a secluded honeymoon and solve all his problems in one fell swoop—tutor her in the ways of etiquette, consummate the marriage as was necessary, perhaps even win her over so that he no longer needed to play such games to keep her in line.

When they returned to the palace in a week's time, she would be a different woman. And he would have everything he wanted. Because once she was perfect, his grandfather would step down, and Frediano would have his control.

"You are my wife. The marriage will be consummated." He smiled at her, enjoying the war he saw on her face—desire and knowledge, want and disgust.

At least he wasn't alone.

"But not until you are ready."

"I will never be ready," she returned, fiercely. With all that fire he denied himself.

"Never is quite the tempt of fate." And then, he left her, his control a tiny thread. But he had held on.

He always would.

CHAPTER SEVEN

ILARIA HAD ALLOWED herself the foolish impulse to cry herself to sleep that night.

Frediano had taken everything away from her—down to the belief she'd get out of this. Even with Sophia free, she could hardly turn her back on the money the Prince offered for her farm, her village. There was no return to her old life.

She had no choices. No options.

So she cried in all the ways she never would've back home, because someone would have heard. Worried.

Here, it didn't matter if she sobbed and wailed or pounded her fists against the wall. *Nothing* mattered.

And amid all of this unfairness was an incomprehensible war of desire and sense. Even alone in her bed, she wanted to relive Frediano's punishing, exciting kiss over and over again. When he spoke of consummating the marriage…she wanted to know what it would be like. Her body felt alive with fire and a reckless restlessness.

No one had ever prepared her for such a confusing war with herself. No matter how she told herself he was the enemy, she wanted him.

But once she was all cried out, she realized this uncharacteristic bout of self-pity felt…cathartic. Her eyes burned and her nose hurt from blowing it. Her temples throbbed, but it was like all that release allowed her to think clearly.

There was no way out, so it was time to accept her fate and make the best of it. It wasn't so different than death. She hadn't wanted to lose anyone she loved, but she had.

She hadn't wanted to lose her life, but she had.

So now she had to find a way to live in this one.

Which meant avoiding being alone with Frediano at all costs. She would never, *ever* willingly go to his bed, give him his heirs. She would never, *ever* let him kiss her as he had last night again.

Or so her brain insisted, while her body relived that moment. His mouth, harsh and demanding, and yet an invitation to some dark pleasure she'd never dreamed of. The way he had touched her. The taste of him, rich and intoxicating. She had never known want at all. So much so that she had been quite sure she would happily live out the rest of her days running her farm and helping her village, with that being all the love and desire she ever needed.

It made no sense, to want nothing to do with a man except feel his body atop hers.

When she finally slept, it was the deep sleep of exhaustion—physical and emotional. She awoke, not to the sounds of people in her room, or to daylight, but to a relentless dark. She looked over at the mobile she'd left on the nightstand.

On a sigh, she grabbed it. If she was to accept her fate, there was one person she still needed to talk to. She dialed Sophia's number, braced for an "Inbox full" message. But to her surprise, Sophia finally answered.

"Ilaria?"

"Sophia. Finally."

"Oh, Ilaria! I'm so sorry I haven't had a chance to call you back. My phone died and everything has been such a tangle. But it's all right now."

Ilaria stared at the ornate room that was not hers and did not speak her thoughts aloud. *How will this ever be all right?* "So, you are well? And free?"

"Yes. It was scary when the border guards stopped us, but then they let us go. My father has tried to find me, but Tino is so clever, we've mostly managed to go under the radar. And now we're officially married, so it doesn't matter."

"Good."

"And…you've married the Prince," Sophia said, sounding a little uncertain, but forging on nonetheless. "I'm sure you can keep us safe since you're the Princess now."

A spurt of something hot and confusing shot through Ilaria, like a blade. She could not speak for a moment, so consumed by it.

It was anger. She didn't want it. She didn't *like* it. Sophia was soft. Pampered. She needed help and protection. It should give Ilaria yet another cause. A sense of purpose and satisfaction. Her position could continue to help Sophia.

But what about me?

For some reason Frediano's words from last night played back in her head. *It sounds as though, much like my parents, your grandfather left you to the wolves.*

But what Frediano did not understand was that some people were not strong enough to fight the wolves, and so some people were needed to step in and help. In all things, she tended and protected her sheep—be they actual livestock or those she loved. No matter what it cost of herself.

What was done was done, and there was no point in *feeling* anything about it. "It's fine."

"You are the most wonderful cousin in the entire world," Sophia gushed. "And a princess now! Isn't that amazing?"

Ilaria could not find words. *Sophia* had not wanted to be a princess, so why did she expect Ilaria would want to be one? Why had Sophia not asked if Ilaria was okay? Ilaria had always considered her cousin sweet and in need of protecting, but in this moment she felt nothing but...

Betrayed.

"A million thank-yous will never be enough, Ilaria, but I have to go now. Tino and I are having a bit of a honeymoon breakfast." She laughed, actually laughed, and Ilaria could not find the words to say goodbye. So, when Sophia said them, Ilaria merely clicked End.

She should be thrilled. So happy for her cousin who now had everything she wanted. She should be satisfied her uncle could not get his title now. She should feel so many good things.

Instead she felt empty. And so very much alone.

Not long after the call with Sophia, the staff began to arrive. They got the fire in the hearth going. They set out clothes and makeup and all the things they would poke and prod her with until she was deemed acceptable.

Ilaria sat where she was in the bed and watched the flames flicker and dance. She did not allow herself to think of home. If she did, she might crumble.

And she could not to do that, because the farm still depended on her. It could run without her, as all the messages she'd received with updates told her, but they needed the money Frediano had promised. And they needed the legitimacy she could offer as Princess, should anyone ever get wind of the fact they did not have guardianship over their minor orphans.

"Is everything all right, Your Highness?"

Ilaria forced herself to smile at Noemi. "Of course." She slid out of the bed and took the robe Aurora handed her. "What is on the schedule for today?"

Noemi's smile was forced, at best. "I believe the Prince would like to inform you of the schedule himself."

Ilaria knew that meant she wouldn't like what was coming, but that was hardly a surprise. Nothing coming would be *good*. So how did she make the best of it? "Noemi... Do you think I will be able to learn enough to prove to the King I can follow protocol before this dinner?"

Noemi seemed to give this some thought, which Ilaria appreciated.

"You seem very determined, Your Highness. I think you can do almost anything you put your mind to."

Though Ilaria had never felt she needed outside reinforcement or assurance, it was nice to hear someone say it. "Thank you, Noemi."

Noemi herded her over to the chair and the hairdresser came over and began to brush while Noemi hovered just out of the way.

"You are very kind, Princess," Noemi continued. "Very warm. I think you will be a great asset to Vantonella. The King and Prince are both honorable and good, but the troubles of their lives have left them…"

"Cold?" Ilaria replied, rather than argue about their *honor*.

"I was going to say reserved, but I can see as how that would come across as cold. Regardless of what it is, you have the warmth to change that. Your speech was so well received. You will be an excellent role model for the young people of Vantonella." Noemi smiled at her in the mirror.

Ilaria managed to smile back. She had no desire to bring warmth to those men. Wasn't sure she believed it possible. But it reminded her that in this little prison she'd somehow gotten herself locked in, there were things to accomplish. The idea she could be a role model…

It was humbling, and an opportunity to help. To be of service.

And by doing so, forget about the loneliness and emptiness that had plagued her after her call with Sophia.

* * *

Everything was prepared. Frediano had instructed Il-aria's staff to pack her things, and to get her ready to fly to the most remote royal residence the crown had to offer. It was Frediano's favorite escape, and like it had when he was a boy, the remote and hidden chalet would serve the crown's purposes.

His grandfather had wholeheartedly approved of Frediano's plan—or at least King Carlo's version of *wholehearted.* But approval did not matter, only the result would.

If he could polish Ilaria into the graceful, proper princess he had promised his grandfather, King Carlo would step down and take care of his health after the wedding dinner.

Frediano would have a week to turn Ilaria into the triumph he'd decided she would be.

It would require more than control. It would require balance. Ilaria would not be bested by threats and de-mands. She had not been raised with the appropriate deference to the crown, or perhaps to anyone, if the pic-ture he was getting of her was correct.

A young woman who was used to being in charge. Taking care of all around her. Good qualities for a queen, he supposed, if she learned her place and used those attributes at the right time.

He would teach her. He would soften her to him. He would bed her where he could indulge himself in all his wildest wants, and then he would be cured of the distraction of his attraction to her. Perhaps having her wouldn't cure him of *wanting* her, but it would certainly help.

It was always easier to resist the temptation you knew, over the one you did not.

He told himself all these things, and still the sight of her landed like a blow. She was not dressed in yesterday's beige, but in black. The dress was not revealing in any way, but the soft-looking material clung to the shape of her. Her staff had done her makeup so that she looked demure, but those mountain witch eyes could not be contained by soft pastels and an innocent neckline.

She eyed the small plane he stood next to with suspicion. "Where are we going?"

"Our honeymoon, of course."

She turned that skeptical look on him. "I do not think that is necessary or wise."

"It is both, Princess. Away from the palace you will have the space to learn the necessary etiquette without distractions. The chalet will allow a more relaxed atmosphere. Perhaps we can even get to know each other. Put all this nasty business behind us."

She stiffened, her chin coming up, and her eyes flashing as he'd hoped they might. "The nasty business where you forced me into a marriage neither of us want?"

"And yet you've already profited from such a match. Just today I spoke with your woman in charge. Vita, is it?"

"Yes," she replied through gritted teeth.

"She expressed the need for some home repairs and expansion, as your cottages are apparently very cramped. I've instructed my staff to take care of this at once."

"It will be a great improvement for many deserving individuals." She also said this through her clenched jaw, but she did not attempt to hurl any insults or argue with him.

He tilted his head and examined her. "Are you feeling all right, Princess? Perhaps you had trouble sleeping."

Her gaze jerked to his for only a second, before she schooled the shocked guilt back into something more placid.

"Ah, so you did," he murmured. "Interesting."

"I assure you, it is not interesting in the least," she returned. "Should we go?"

He did not move. He was not used to someone aside from his grandfather trying to order him about. "If you did not have trouble sleeping, perhaps it was dreams that plagued you. Maybe you'd like to share them."

She did not look up at him this time. She kept her gaze on the plane. "I dreamt of bloody coups," she returned, then flashed him a sarcastic smile.

It shocked him to his core that he wanted to laugh at that, which was decidedly *not* funny. It was best to get on with this. The sooner he won her over, the better.

He offered his arm. "Come."

She reluctantly placed her hand there, all the while studying the plane they walked toward. She hesitated at the bottom of the stair. When Frediano raised an eyebrow, she shook her head and continued inside. It was small so it was capable of landing on the small, mountain airstrip near the chalet, but no less luxurious than a larger plane.

The seating was plush and comfortable, and he had often worked the short flight as though he were sitting in his office at the palace. He took his usual seat, but she still stood there, awkwardly holding on to a purse.

"I've never been on a plane," she finally said, though he wondered if she knew she'd said it out loud.

"Does the idea of flying frighten you?"

She blinked at the question, then looked out the window, though they hadn't left the ground yet but were only taxiing. "I don't think so. I'd certainly rather try this than speak in front of all those people again."

"You will need to work on that."

Her gaze jerked back to his. She even opened her mouth as if ready for a tart rejoinder, but then she closed her mouth, smoothed out her expression and seemed to consider her seating options.

She settled herself into a chair across from him. She still clutched her purse at her abdomen, but she crossed her legs and he found his gaze drawn to the alluring line of her calf. Would her skin taste like her mouth, crushed wildflowers and wild storms?

He lifted his gaze to meet hers. If she'd noticed his interested perusal, she did not show it. Her mouth was screwed up in a kind of frustrated frown. He did not allow himself to consider the fact that kissing her had not lessened his desire to do so. *Knowing* how she reacted to him did not abate any of the lust coursing through his body.

"Do you honestly intend this farce to go on forever?" she asked abruptly.

The question did not anger him as maybe it should, because she seemed…not exactly lost. She was too self-assured for lost. But perhaps…vulnerable, and it poked at some unknown soft place inside of him he'd rather not acknowledge existed. "I'm afraid it must."

"But why? I realize an annulment or a divorce might cause a bit of gossip, but surely nothing as scandalous as your parents got up to." She flinched a little, as if she expected him to react to what was only the truth.

He had already considered these options, of course. He'd considered them that first night in the cathedral when she'd announced her identity. But it was impossible.

He could not imagine going back then or now for many reasons. The main one, of course, was his grandfather's health. It would take time to find another acceptable bride, time neither of them had. Not to mention his grandfather's reaction to reversing course, and the possibility of the press catching wind.

So it could not be done. "It is out of the question."

She heaved out a sigh. But she did not ask any more questions. She clutched her bag, harder and harder as the plane gained speed and then flung itself into the air.

He enjoyed watching her reactions as they flew. So much that he did not do any of the work he'd been planning. He simply sat and observed as she leaned closer and closer to the window until he finally suggested she move to the window seat.

She hadn't even argued.

There was something so honest about her. None of the artifice he'd grown up with—both his parents and the rich and titled who glittered and gossiped and cared more about that than the good of the country.

Now her nose was practically pressed to the window as they began their descent into the mountains. He heard her breath catch. It was easy to see Ilaria was impressed by a pretty place. Because the Montellero chalet might not have been as big as the palace back in Roletto, but it was a masterpiece of wood and mostly glass nestled into the side of a mountain. Private. Secluded. Perfect for his ends.

And he would remember his own ends above all else.

CHAPTER EIGHT

ILARIA WONDERED IF she'd ever get used to the finery, the sheer beauty of everything in Frediano's world. The chalet was...well, she couldn't use the term *fairy tale* because this was no fairy tale. It was a very opulent prison.

Without escape, apparently.

But as Frediano helped her down from the plane, and then into the car that would take them from airstrip to chalet, it was hard to feel that drumbeat of panic. In some ways, this secluded little hideaway felt like home. The mountains, the blue sky, the cool air. There was only a small staff waiting for them, so that it was almost like they were alone.

The chalet was beautiful and luxurious. The structure seemed to be made almost entirely of glass, with only the necessary wooden beams to hold it together. No doubt inside you could look anywhere and see the beautiful scenery of the Alps around them.

Everything she had decided this morning and on the flight here felt solidified somehow. Noemi saying she could be a role model had started it, but there had been something about looking out the plane window, the world below them like a miniature on display. It had been exhilarating, the closest to a bird she'd ever be. And in that simple joy of flying she'd decided that joy *was* within her power.

Even if little else was.

She would learn the etiquette. Even with as little education as she'd had, she knew that a woman needed to learn the rules in order to break them effectively.

Frediano had been trying to intimidate her earlier when he'd mentioned speaking to Vita and arranging improvements at the farm. He wanted her to feel as though he pulled all the strings. But he'd only given her an idea.

No doubt Roletto orphanages and workhouses needed the same kind of improvements her farm did. No doubt there were trusts and scholarships and whatever else to be created to benefit the orphans of Estraz and other disasters. She would work tirelessly to dedicate her life not to the palace or the King—whether that be Carlo or Frediano. She would dedicate her life to the *people*, just as she'd promised them on that balcony yesterday.

And because thinking of things she could *do* reminded her that she had *some* kind of power now, even if it wasn't the freedom she'd hoped for, she was determined to get everything *she* wanted out of this week.

Frediano craved a biddable, boring wife. Perhaps part of her wanted to rebel at that as a matter of course, but she was smarter than that. Or perhaps she'd just never had the luxury to rebel.

The bottom line was, it did not matter what Frediano

wanted. She didn't mind appearing biddable and boring if it suited *her* purposes, because this wasn't about thwarting *him*. He was a prince. Powerful and in line to be the King. There was no sense beating her head against the brick wall of trying to best him. He'd only change the rules and declare himself winner.

But she could focus on making herself happy. On doing things that would help those *she* cared about. Frediano was simply…an overzealous hound. He would bark at her and herd her into the little path he created, and she—somehow being the sheep in this scenario—would do what she pleased all the same.

"I will show you to your room," Frediano said. "You may rest, then you will change for dinner. We will begin our first lesson then. The staff is limited here, as we have managed to keep the location of this property secret for decades." He led her into a hallway that wasn't glass, but instead cozily constructed of dark woods decorated in various artworks depicting the mountains.

"This is your room," he said, turning the knob and opening the door. But he stood in such a way he blocked her entrance. "I trust you can dress yourself for dinner?" he asked, innocently enough.

There was *nothing* innocent about the comment, she knew full well. Simply from the way her blood heated at the light in his eyes. She reminded herself he was a hound or brick wall—one she would never succumb to—but she couldn't keep all her sarcasm at bay. "I think you know I have survived all these years without help in that department."

His eyes took a long, slow tour of her body, his mouth

curving ever so slightly. Giving the strangest appearance of softness when she knew there was no softness to this man. And still she ached for something from him she did not fully understand.

"I would be happy to offer my services to help you undress," he said, and it was something like a purr. The low, resonant tones that had, from the very beginning, affected her in a deep, intimate way.

She knew, despite all her inexperience, just *what* he was suggesting. It should make her angry.

But he held her gaze and she was reminded far too vividly of last night. The feel of his tongue sliding against hers, his hands, the hardness of his body she was crushed to. The heat pulsing at her core.

She should look away, leave, *do* something. She was certain she would. Any minute. Instead of letting all those memories of last night crowd around her. Instead of finding her breath harder and harder to manage. Instead of relishing the waves of sensation battering her as she relived every second of last night.

Not that long ago, she had believed she would be quite happy never experiencing what happened between a man and a woman. She had too much to do around the farm and with the orphans to worry about the needs of a partner.

But these past few days the thought had consumed her. To the point it crowded out the things she had once believed immovable in their weight and importance in her mind.

Frediano had moved out of the way, giving her a clear escape into her room.

She did not take it.

Instead, she stood where she was, certainly flushed and breathing too heavily to hide her reaction to him. He took her hand then, turned it over as if to study her palm. He'd called her hands rough, and though she hadn't done her normal chores in a few days, they were as rough as they had been. Even the palace could not scrape away all her years of labor.

He lifted her hand and held her gaze as he brushed his mouth across her knuckles. "My room is at the end of this hall. Feel free to join me there. Whenever you wish."

There was a moment, such a strange moment, when it seemed like the most sensible course of action. Her body ached for him. He would no doubt show her *some* kind of pleasure, if a simple touch, a simple look could do this much. And then she would know all those things she'd assumed she never would.

But she did not love him, and even if her body understood the need and wants of the act, she had always assumed *love* was part of that. It was supposed to be, she was almost sure of it.

"I will *never* wish it," she said, but it was not the firm statement she'd hoped for. If anything it was breathless, almost whispered, and though she'd said the correct words, she couldn't help but feel as if her *never* sounded a lot like *please*.

He smiled, but he dropped her hand. "*Never* make promises you can't keep, *tesoro*."

Frediano studied the small dinner table the staff had put together. It was arranged as the royal wedding dinner would be, if on a smaller scale. At this very table, King Carlo had once carefully and patiently taken Frediano through everything he would need to know to be a prince, and so now Frediano would do the same for Ilaria.

My wife.

She had much to learn, and he wasn't convinced she was all that eager to, even with his generous donation to her little farm. He'd thought it would be simple enough to use his money and power—that was what most women in his acquaintance were interested in, after all—to give her what she wanted.

He would need to delve deeper. Learn more about her to better understand her. And once he understood her, it would be easy enough to consummate the marriage and then return to the palace with his obedient bride in tow.

Satisfied with this plan, pushing away all the doubts that had plagued him as *nothing* with Ilaria had gone according to plan, he waited for her to arrive.

He glanced at his watch, expecting the time to be later than it was. Instead, he was ready early, like some eager schoolboy.

He supposed he was eager. Eager to solve the problem that was Ilaria. She mystified him. He did not know people whose causes weren't themselves, outside of his grandfather, who, like him, lived for Vantonella and upholding the Monetellero name.

Surely Ilaria could not be as good and charitable as she behaved. There had to be some flaw there, and he needed to find it.

He heard her footsteps before she appeared. Normally, he would not turn to look at her. He would have stood still, staring at the window wall and the glorious mountains his parents had thought they could tame, and waited until she was either compelled to speak or make *some* noise.

But this week was not about *him*. It was about getting to the bottom of Ilaria, and if she was not a woman won over by orders and bribes, he would have to attempt something wholly out of character.

Softness. He wasn't sure he knew what that looked like, but he would try. Had to try. He would stop at nothing to get what he needed from her.

So he turned as she entered the room from the hallway. He smiled at her. She was dressed modestly and somewhat casually in dark slacks and a soft red sweater that clung to her generous curves.

She did something to him and Frediano did not know how to stop it. But he would. By the end of this week, he would. If he had to learn her inside and out, glut himself on her until there was nothing left between them. Whatever it took, he would do.

"When you approach a member of the royal family, you are to curtsy," he said, and not as an order but as a *gentle* reminder. He even smiled encouragingly at her.

"Am I not a member of the royal family?" she returned, smiling at him with a kind of bland politeness that crawled under his skin.

He did not falter. "You are, indeed, which means your curtsy must be infallible. Beauty and grace defined in a simple movement."

"A deferential movement," she returned.

"A symbol of respect," he countered. "Just as I bow to my grandfather."

"But I do not respect you, and I respect your grandfather even less." She held his gaze as if what she said didn't border on treason.

He clenched his teeth together. He had promised himself he would not be provoked. If he responded in anger, in frustration, and the biting sarcasm she seemed to drag out of him, he would not accomplish his goals.

"Be that as it may," he said, his tone carefully neutral, each syllable a hard-won battle against his temper. "You will need to curtsy to us both upon your entrance to the wedding dinner. If you wish to be an embarrassment at the royal wedding dinner, I suppose that is your choice," he said. Though he didn't mean it. In the slightest.

But she wanted choice, so he would give her the illusion of such.

She took a deep breath and seemed to shake something within herself. She smiled at him and then preformed a curtsy that was—if not totally beautiful or graceful or natural-looking—very nearly suitable. "I assure you, Your Highness, I am eager to take all the instruction I can get."

She said this with a sweet smile, the picture-perfect version of the wife he'd wanted.

He didn't trust it. Still, he gestured toward the table. Maybe this brief respite from ill will would allow them to cover some ground. "At any meal with the royal family, you will wait to be seated until your husband or king pulls out a chair for you." Frediano moved forward, pulled out a chair and gestured Ilaria toward it.

He watched as she very clearly attempted not to look at him as she took the offered seat, but at the last second her gaze met his. He did not understand the sheer chaos that went on inside of him when she looked at him.

Chaos was not an option, even here in the secluded mountain chalet. So he released her seat and moved stiffly to his, across the table from her.

He gestured for Como to pour the wine, much the same as would be done at their wedding dinner, though with more people on both sides.

"While the wine is poured, we will engage in small talk with those around us. So…how is your cousin?" he asked.

"Married and quite happy," she replied. She muttered something after that clear response. It sounded an awful lot like *no thanks to you*.

"I suppose she thanked you profusely for biting the bullet." That wasn't exactly *small talk*, but he was intrigued by her reaction to her cousin now that Sophia was free. And Ilaria was stuck.

Before, Ilaria had spoken of her cousin brazenly. Like the warrior protecting her village from all who wished to do them harm. There was a moment here before all that zeal returned.

"She did thank me. And hoped I could continue to keep her safe from her father. Because that is the kind of man your grandfather trusts. The kind of men who make their grown daughters terrified."

A dark jolt of old pain landed deep in Frediano's gut.

A pain he'd have sworn he'd excised some time ago. But her scenario reminded him of a question that had plagued him in his darkest hours as a teenager trying to earn his grandfather's respect and trust.

How long would he have been a prisoner to his parents' whims if they had not died? Would he have ever been free of the toxic environment they created wherever they went?

A foolish question because it did not matter. They were dead. And he'd chosen to dedicate his life to everything they'd eschewed. No one's whims, selfish wants or desires would threaten him ever again. Even his own.

"No parent should have such a hold on their child, it is true." He said, frustrated his voice was gruff. It made her look up at him with some of that softness he knew was dangerous. Control could not be wielded if he was weak to her softness. He had to have the upper hand. "But these are personal matters I'm sure my grandfather is unaware of."

That softness disappeared. "I would like to make him aware."

"Revenge, Princess?"

"Justice," she returned, clearly having given this some thought. He had the strangest sensation that perhaps she was playing him this evening the same as he was playing her. He did not know what she sought— except perhaps the upper hand.

Maybe he could give her that illusion as well.

He explained the layout of the royal table, how she would be expected to proceed through the dinner. Staff came in with the first course, then the second. Ilaria really did know nothing of etiquette, but he remembered being in the same position. His grandfather had been endlessly patient with him, so Frediano showed the same kind of patience to his wife.

She seemed to be trying, enough that she insisted on resetting her place and then going over the different silverware and glasses once more. It was strange to find himself smiling as she succeeded. To feel proud at how quickly she caught on. He appreciated her tenacity. Her inability to let failure stand.

He studied her as dessert was served. He need not be *impressed* by her, he needed to get to the bottom of her. Revenge on her uncle? He could aid in that. The success of her farm and legitimacy of her orphans without legal guardians? He'd already handled that so long as she met his conditions. But he needed to know her, inside and out, so that she never surprised him. So that his life was in his control alone.

And, of course, present his grandfather with a perfect princess so King Carlo would step down from the throne and take care of his health.

"While all these dinners I'm sure will be beautiful and luxurious, what I'd really like to do is discuss how the palace intends to help those without such luxuries." She met his gaze across the table as she lifted a fork to her lips.

He watched her enjoy the crostata and wondered if she knew her eyes fluttered closed for a moment, and she let out a sigh, just a quiet one, in pleasure.

"You seem to enjoy these luxuries," he said, smiling. He rather enjoyed watching her eat. Watching her forget herself for these small moments.

She did not smile in return. Instead, she put her fork down. "I would happily abstain if I thought it might lead to change. In fact—"

"Your point is taken, Ilaria. You wish your role as princess to be a voice of the people." There was so much that could go wrong there, but there had to be a way to give her the illusion of what she craved, while controlling it all the same. "This is possible, of course. The crown is involved in many charitable efforts."

"Are they?"

"Yes, my grandfather is a patron to many causes. His greatest efforts are in education outreach and historical preservation. Many of our dukes also offer patronages. Military, social services, the arts. Et cetera."

"What about you?" Ilaria asked, studying him.

"Me?"

"Yes, what are you a patron of?"

"It is of no matter." He took a sip of his wine, considering. He had no doubt she would approve of his patronages. But he worried it would allow her too much insight into him. Still, it was public record, and perhaps his personal interests would even soften the philanthropic Ilaria to him.

"It is of *some* matter, as I am interested."

"Very well. I lend my name to many medical organizations. Hospitals, particularly those that cater to children whose families cannot afford or do not care enough to provide treatment for their children."

She frowned, clearly surprised that he might share

an interest. "But this is just your name. Signing a check or cutting a ribbon. I don't want to just be a symbol or a voice. I want to *help* people."

He could tell her, of course. That he often volunteered hours, so long as it could be kept away from the press's prying eyes, as he wished for none of the attention his parents had gotten for just what Ilaria had outlined. He could inform her of the long hours he spent working with accounting departments, fundraising efforts, and the like.

But this felt a step too far. So he lifted his wineglass and studied it, before sliding his gaze to her once more. "Isn't it funny how often helping others leads us directly to our own peril? After all, if you had not stuck your nose into your cousin's problems, you would not have been in the cathedral that night."

There was a moment when he could see he'd clearly caught her off guard, but she recovered swiftly. "While that is a nice fantasy, how could I have been happy knowing my cousin would have been sentenced to a life she didn't want?"

He sipped, set his glass down. "Your cousin seems happy enough with *you* in such a situation."

She paled. As if that thought had not crossed her mind, and perhaps she really was this virtuous. Maybe, despite tragedy, she was so unaccustomed to betrayal she did not recognize it until it was pointed out to her.

"Helping is always the right thing to do," she said, but her voice was small. "One would think the future leader of our country might have more interest in honor." She was trying to regain that strength of purpose, but clearly him pointing out Sophia did not care much for her happiness had taken the wind out of her sails.

"Honor and sacrificing yourself for the needs of others are two very different things, Ilaria."

"Most of us not raised in palaces and with silver spoons shoved in our mouths are taught that *honor* is helping others, being of service to those who *cannot* return the favor."

"At the expense of yourself? What of you, Ilaria? You have suffered tragedy. Don't you deserve some of this help you're always doling out?" He spread his arms to encompass the room. "You are no longer a poor little sheep herder. You are a princess and, yes, you can help all those you wish to help. Easily. In the snap of a finger, really. But what is it *you* want?"

"To help. That is all I need," she said, nodding firmly. "Noemi said that I can be a good role model. If I cannot be free to return to my life, and I feel that after that ridiculous introduction even if it were possible, it would be different, then I must make the best of the one I have. If I can be a role model, if I can help those who have, as you said, suffered tragedy, then that is what I will do."

"A good monarch can always be a model of some kind." His parents, after all, had taught him what *not* to do. "Service is part of this, of course. But that does not mean you must be a martyr to these causes. That you cannot have your own wants." He gestured at the dessert she'd stopped eating. "And have them be fulfilled."

This was clearly not what she wanted to hear, and he was surprised at how much this angered her. He'd expected her to have something at the ready that he could fulfill. A list of desires as his princess that he would happily give her if it guaranteed her obedience.

Most people in his acquaintance only required a bribe or a threat to behave accordingly. Their wants met, and then they were easily controlled.

Instead, she was silently smoldering. Her eyes turning a deeper shade of green, her cheeks flushing with color. No doubt if he reached over and touched her pulse it would be racing.

He wanted to make it race for completely different reasons. To mold that anger into passion. All this talk of *wants* made it impossible to not think of his own. And in this moment, as he watched her, they all centered on *her*. His wants were dangerous, always, but here, where he could control everything, he could indulge in this one.

"All right, then," she said, leaning forward, temper flashing in her eyes. If he believed in bewitching, he would say that all spells started in their changeable green depths. What would it be like to sink himself into all that magic?

He needed to know. So that once they returned to the palace, he could fight it. He could *control* it.

"If there are some special wants I'm supposed to have for myself, do tell, what is it *you* want, Frediano?"

He rather enjoyed the way she bit out his name. As if it were a curse. He supposed it was perverse of him, but no doubt her passion was like her anger—bright and sharp and dangerous.

He considered his wine, and then her. It would not be tonight, but that didn't mean he couldn't begin the seduction.

"This evening, *tesoro*, the only thing I want is you."

CHAPTER NINE

ILARIA SUCKED IN a breath and cursed herself that she could not be more worldly and handle such direct overtures without reaction. But he spoke those simple words with all that concentrated focus on *her*, and it felt as if her lungs had seized up and no longer worked properly.

Because the terrible truth was, she wanted him, too. It was the only want she could think of, when pinned underneath that dark, intense gaze.

She had to clear her throat to speak. "I do not *like* you. I will certainly never love you." Though it had been hard to hold on to her hate for him when he spoke of his parents. Clearly they had neglected him, and though he had tried to speak of his patronages with some detachment, she knew, the moment he'd spoken of families who did not care enough to afford their children treatment, that the cause was personal to him.

Could it be that under all his hard, domineering, demanding ways, there was kindness? She'd seen flashes of it herself. The way he spoke to his aide as though they were friends, the breathing technique he'd offered in the midst of her panic, and his softness toward his grandfather.

She hated to admit it, but Frediano was not *all* bad.

But he certainly made her feel things she did not know how to navigate.

"Desire does not need to be about like or *love*, *tesoro*," he said with a lazy shrug—when she was quite certain he'd never been lazy. "In my experience, few people love anything more than they love themselves."

"Your experience depresses me," she said. She desperately tried *not* to think of the story he'd told her about his parents after his swim, all the anger he held toward them. Because though she'd told him it did not make her pity him…it did. When she didn't harden her heart against it.

Too well she could picture a little boy, the pawn of reckless, selfish people who did not love him and then raised by a cold, detached grandfather who seemed to have only impressed *duty* upon him. If she gave room for those thoughts, for seeing the personal connection beneath his patronages, she understood why he might have become the remote, uncompromising man before her. And she sympathized. It made her see him as more than just the cold, authoritarian enemy.

Her father and grandfather had not been perfect. The more years she lived, the more she understood their flaws, where they'd failed her.

And yet, they had loved her. She never once doubted that. It made all the difference. People could not be perfect, but if they loved… Well, it could be forgiven.

Who loved Frediano?

It does not matter. He is the villain in this story.

"What is love to you, Ilaria?" the Prince demanded. "Someone as inexperienced as yourself, who had never even kissed a man before. Your mother died when you were born, so you did not have your parents' shining example of love and devotion to hold up as an impossible paragon to reach." He spoke with such sarcasm, as if love and devotion were fake and fairy tales. Things to be criticized.

She wanted it to stir her temper once more, but it only made her sadder for him. "My parents loved each other. I may not have seen it, but my father spoke of it. My grandfather and father loved me and each other. Perhaps I have not experienced romantic love, but I know love because I have felt it."

"And yet you did not marry or have babies. You dedicated your life to saving your cousin from marrying me."

She looked at him for a moment, truly looked at him—the man behind her abduction and forced wedding, the man behind the facade. She didn't want to, but when he spoke of important things, all she could see were the wounds underneath his carefully placed masks.

Because clearly he did not understand—could not *fathom* the truth. "Don't you see? That was love, too." She had the strangest desire to reach out and put her hand over his. She quelled the urge, but she could not resist the words of truth. "When you love someone, you are willing to sacrifice for them."

"That sounds even more a tragedy than most of the love stories I have heard." He pushed back in his chair and stood. He skirted the table and moved next to her, hand outstretched. "Now it is time for your next lesson."

When she recoiled, he laughed. The sound was dark and deep, and it danced along her skin like a misty morning rain shower in the mountains. She craved more of it, because it was something close to happiness… and nothing about Frediano had ever seemed particularly happy.

It would not do to think about why that was. To allow this feeling of empathy for him to soften her toward him, when there would never be any return tenderness.

"You must learn to dance, Princess. And not a charming country reel. A proper, royal waltz."

His hand remained outstretched, and she supposed because she was so busy feeling sorry for him, wondering about his *happiness*, she didn't think the movement through and slid her hand into his without bracing herself.

So it was a jolt, that no doubt he felt, too. Of all that *want* she kept claiming she didn't have. Because if there was anything she wanted for herself and only herself, it was to discover where all these feelings could lead.

She should be more afraid of that than she was.

He pulled her to her feet and then led her away from the table and into the living room lit by the crackling fire in the hearth and the moon that shone through the glass, and the stars that glittered like jewels.

It felt almost as if they were outside. There was something so familiar about it, like the sky back home.

She should know better than to relax, but the comforting scene conspired against her to ease the tension in her shoulders. He played no music as he slid his hand around her back, his other still holding her hand.

He explained the steps as he moved her through them. She tried to pay attention to memorizing them. She had no interest in dancing, but less interest in looking a fool. So she *tried* to focus on the simple one-two-three rhythm. On moving her feet where they should go.

But her mind kept drifting to the large hand secure at the small of her back. To the slight friction every time their bodies brushed. To the size of his other hand, which held hers.

She didn't dare look anywhere but at her feet—both for fear she'd stumble or step on his, and because if she glanced up... She wasn't sure how she would look away. How she would dance knowing what his intense gaze did to her.

This was all very dangerous footing, and she had to save herself from all that danger. Somehow.

"You must memorize the steps enough you look at me, Princess. Not your feet."

Ilaria kept her eyes firmly on her shoes. "I think you expect too much of me."

"By all accounts, this is impossible. Your story is one of resilience, intelligence and determination. Surely you can learn a little dance."

She lifted her gaze in surprise because he sounded sincere. She knew he couldn't be if he was complimenting her, but when she looked at his dark eyes there was none of that biting censure, and the cruel line of his mouth was vaguely curved.

As though she…impressed him in some way. As though there could be a softness hidden in this man.

"Let me lead you," he said, and it almost sounded *gentle*. So gentle she found herself obeying without even thinking of it. He took her through the steps again, and she let him move her. Though there was no music around them, she felt some new tune inside of herself and swayed to the beat of it under his steady, dark gaze.

"See what can happen if you trust me?"

It was frightening to feel this way, to feel powerless, when her whole life had been about finding power in all the places she had none. She needed to reclaim some piece of that. "I could never trust you."

"So many *nevers*," he said, his silky smooth voice sounding wholly unbothered, when she'd expected anger or frustration. He pulled her closer, so that their legs were pressed together and her chest was crushed to his, and between them she could feel the hard, surprisingly large length of him pressed up against her. "A shame, but I shall endeavor to carry on. We cannot always get what we want."

She felt as if he'd pulled the floor out from under her—again. She could rebuild, she always did, but not when he held her. Not when his voice shivered through her. She couldn't find her footing.

"Some people never get what they want," she shot back at him, not sure where the words came from. Surely not from her. Her grandfather had always taught her to be grateful for what they had, no matter how little. Because it could always get worse. And had, so often.

So she was grateful for her health. That her grandfather had been able to live to see her become an adult even if her parents had not. She was even grateful for the chance to save Sophia. She *was*, because it meant she'd done the right thing.

Love was sacrifice, and so she loved. And sacrificed. Over and over again.

Who loves you now that everyone who loved you is dead? Now that you have given Sophia exactly what she wanted? It was a voice that sounded strangely like Frediano's, when he'd uttered no such words. Not that the words he spoke were any more comforting.

"Some people never get what they want?" Frediano asked. "Or *you* never get what you want?"

It felt too close to a truth she didn't want to look at. There would be nothing left if she couldn't hold on to those old beliefs. "I loved my life, until I was tricked into marrying someone."

"Did you?"

"Yes, and I will endeavor to find a way to love this one. To be grateful for it." She tried to pull away from him, but he held her firm. So she stilled and met his gaze with a fierce one of her own. "Because as you once told me, Frediano, the world is cruel and it does not care what becomes of me. But I care. So I will always seek to find the good."

"By always being complacent with the situation in front of you?" His words were calm, but his eyes flashed. "Without ever wanting more than what little you have?"

She did not know why he kept saying things that

seemed to twist her heart into knots. That landed like little avalanches. Painful and feeling so sharply true when there was no way it could be true. "I want to help people."

"So you say, but that is not all. Your body wants me, even if your heart does not." He pressed his mouth to the skin just under her jaw and though she tried to strengthen herself against it, she shuddered in response.

"Allow me to give you something you want, Ilaria," he murmured. And there was none of the usual steel in his voice. It was warmth and entreaty. The subtle, drugging use of persuasion. "I promise you, there is no need for love. Pleasure is enough."

Pleasure. It already arced through her like a live wire. It seemed to slither through her body, getting rid of any resolve or intelligence. So that she was only left with that *want* he kept talking about.

As though he'd hypnotized her into thinking of nothing else.

Right and wrong had always been so clear. She had never understood how anyone could be tempted by the devil when he was evil.

But finally she understood. Temptation. The blinding desire to do something you knew could not be smart or good. And how it eradicated that voice inside that chose the right thing, the smart thing.

So there was no voice. There was only the feel of him, the scent of some expensive cologne, and the flash of his dark eyes. Because he wanted her.

And she wanted him.

* * *

Frediano had not planned this, and he knew that following his desires was a mistake. He'd meant to soften her. To arouse her, yes. But to not give in just yet to his own desires.

The taste of her skin was too much. The tremors he could feel as he held her close. The catch of her breath, the *response*.

She did not push him away, she did not tell him no. Perhaps there was a war inside her, but she did not give in to the side that had refused him before. Not yet.

His hands slid under her shirt, to where she was soft and warm. He ran his palms over her ribs, her breasts over the fabric of her bra. There was no longer the pretense of the dance, there was only his hands on her, her body pressed to his of her own free will.

He did not understand her any more than he understood his desire for her. That anyone could truly be so selfless that her own wants were *confronting*. He wished he could believe her a liar, but there was no evidence. She had wrapped herself up in her own sainthood, in her own sacrifices she called love.

He had never seen love sacrifice, but maybe he'd never seen love. His parents had claimed their love was more important than anything. That it was superior to laws, to the demands of royal life, to the responsibilities of being a parent. But maybe it hadn't been love. Maybe, as in all else, it had only been selfishness and wreckage.

But if love was the opposite—sacrifice and nothing more—what would Frediano want with that, either?

It made no earthly sense why he was even contemplating the nature of love. This was about chemistry. Desire and attraction. It was about the practicalities of consummating the marriage and the process of producing heirs.

And nothing to do with *emotions*.

Her head fell back, and he traveled the line of her neck with his mouth, the sound of her ragged breathing erasing everything except this tide of need.

"Ilaria," he said, savoring each syllable of her name. "What do you want?" he whispered before pressing another kiss just under her ear.

She inhaled sharply, and he waited, here on the brink of madness for her to answer his question.

Because he would not give in until she did. No matter how he wanted, no matter how his control strained, *she* would give in. Her innocence meant she did not know all he could show her, and he would make sure she understood how superior *pleasure* could be to *love and sacrifice*.

She did not answer his question in words. She tilted her head so their mouths were just a breath apart, her eyes an ethereal green in the moonlight and starlight around them. Her eyes betrayed nothing but that luminescent desire.

Then, she leaned forward and kissed him, so untested, but not nervous. That was not who she was.

She had already slayed dragons in her life, time and time again. He wondered if she feared anything at this point, and almost envied her for the courage that so impressed everyone she came into contact with. Her orphans, her neighbors, his staff. Even his grandfather had been *impressed*.

She was a triumph. She would be *his* triumph.

She would be his. Only his.

But there could be no mistake. He eased away from that dangerous mouth, but not to stop this. There was no stopping this.

"Tell me," he ordered. "You will not get to decide I tricked you into this in the morning. This is your choice, *tesoro*. So tell me, what do you want?"

CHAPTER TEN

A CHOICE.

Frediano held her so tightly she was nearly immobile. There was no escape, but the firm grip also didn't allow her to kiss him again. Because she had to choose.

Kissing him had been a choice, but she supposed it had been the coward's choice. Because she hadn't said the words. She'd given in to him.

Giving in to him was not inevitable, no matter how she felt it was, with her body engulfed with a desperate need that had a will of its own.

So she had a choice to make, and whatever it was, she would be the one to live with all the consequences hereafter.

Because she did not love him, and she was under no illusion he loved her, or ever could, considering he did not believe in sacrifice.

But she did not hate him as much as she should. He had revealed too much about what he'd come from for her to *hate* him. How could a cold upbringing create anything other than a cold man? And yes, he'd had far more privileges than she'd ever had, but she knew from experience that a child's financial situation did not change the absence of love. Sophia had not had an easy upbringing simply because her father was alive and rich. Giovanni loved nothing and no one. He had manipulated and emotionally abused his wife and daughter.

Certainly money helped a person, there was no doubt about it, but without love, what did it matter?

Ilaria tried to hold on to the fact that Frediano had forced her into this situation, but if she had decided to make the best of it, how could she hold on to her anger?

All in all, the choice before her now was not a different decision than the one she'd made this morning. That she wouldn't go against him simply to go against him. She would make her own choices, regardless of him. She was supposed to be making the best of her new life. He had introduced the subject of wants. Of getting something *she* wanted. For once.

For once. She looked at his intense, dark eyes, let the heat of him sweep through her. If she let all the outside world go, if she focused only on this and him, there was one clear want.

"I want you," she whispered. It didn't matter that she'd told him *never*, because *this* was what she wanted. To eradicate the distance between them, to have him show her all that dizzying heat they could create.

Maybe it could even be a starting point. Something *good* could come out of it, and if that was the devil whispering what she wanted to hear, well, so be it. For tonight, so be it.

The noise that erupted from him could only be considered a growl. And then *finally* his mouth crashed to hers. Hard and unyielding, fire and need. She threw herself into it. Into him. She melted, yielding softness to demanding hard. His hands molded her body, learning every last inch of her and it did not matter if he touched fabric or flesh, it all burned through her.

He lifted her sweater over her head. Since she had not picked out any of her clothes, down to her underwear, they still did not feel like hers. And so, him taking them off her somehow felt more right than keeping them on.

Because this was her. Her skin, her freckles, her goose bumps. He unclasped her bra, then spread his fingers wide as he smoothed his hands down her back. His wicked mouth traveled down her neck to her chest, wreaking havoc wherever he kissed, licked, sucked.

"Bellissima," he murmured, his hands cupping her breasts. She had the dim thought she should be embarrassed, to be naked at all, let alone in front of such a man. But her body felt alive, as if for the first time. And she wanted something…something out of reach, which she knew he would give her.

"Let me see how much you desire me." He laid her down on the plush rug, the moonlight dancing over them it its own waltz. He undid the snap of her pants and then drew them down over her legs. Until she was lying completely naked on a rug.

Even though he was still dressed, it somehow seemed exactly right when he looked at her like she was a miracle. Like everything he saw was everything he'd ever wanted.

"Ah, such beauty. Such strength. I promise, this will be no sacrifice. Only your pleasure, my princess." His mouth found hers again, and while one hand leveraged him above her, the other traveled down until he found the center of her aching need.

She did not know anything that would happen beyond the basic mechanics of it all, and yet the unknown only seemed to tangle with the dark twist of needs inside of her so that when he touched her, intimately and expertly, she cried out, so surprised by the bolt of pleasure she reached out for him.

And he was there, his mouth on hers. His broad shoulders sturdy. The strength of him a comfort as this wild and fierce passion swept through her and turned her into something else. As he stroked a finger inside of her. *Her.* When he touched her, where she was slick with need, there was nothing else in the world except him.

She said his name in fevered whispers, in desperate moans, as his finger slid inside of her, and she did not recognize the noises she made, the desperation she felt. It was all so new and intense and different. She arched against him, pulled at him to find some way to be closer. To be one.

And there was no shame in that or him. In *this.*

She only felt as though she had finally found joy.

Ilaria was a curse. Perfect in every way, as if she had been designed for him and his every last desire. She was beautiful and strong and glowing underneath the celestial light shining in through the windows.

Touching the molten core of her was not enough. He needed to be inside of her. To consume her, possess her in every way he could. She had enjoyed no lovers before him, and this made her *his*.

His.

She reached out, her fingers fumbling as she worked to undo the buttons of his shirt while he explored her with his fingers. She rid him of his shirt, then trailed her hands down his chest, her hesitant touch as erotic as anything. Until she stopped at his belt.

He paused, watching her eyes flicker from his pants to him. A hint of uncertainty. He wanted her beyond reason, and yet there was something else here. Something painful and twisting in his chest.

But she did not change her mind as he feared. She did not come to her senses. She held his gaze.

"Show me," she said. "Everything."

Everything. So he kissed her long and deep. And she met every kiss, every nip, every thrust of his hand with one of her own. His courageous princess. Until her fingers were digging into his shoulders as she pressed herself so fully against him.

She was arched in perfect offering for him to take her breast deep into his mouth, teasing nipple with tongue until she was panting. Until she was *begging*.

He knew she did not know what exactly she begged for. There was no practiced seduction here. Only her want and her need and her *desperation*. Her *please* echoing in his ears until there was nothing but that.

It soaked into his bloodstream like a drug. Nothing else mattered except *her*, this center of everything. Giving her everything she deserved to find at the hands of her first lover.

Her only.

He stroked her, finding the bundle of nerves that had her crying out and shuddering in his arms. Her release the sweetest nectar he'd ever encountered.

His own breathing was ragged as though he'd run a marathon, but this was only the beginning. The very beginning.

He dragged his tongue down the elegant curve of her neck. He sampled her skin like the delicacy it was. She was warmth, sunlight after a long, dreary winter. Hope after nothing but disappointment. The taste of something forbidden and irresistible.

And he could not content himself with only this. He needed her. All of her. Now. No more waiting, no more torture. No more long nights haunted by those green eyes. He freed himself and her eyes met his, wild with desire.

He knew she would not refuse him, saw all the ways she wanted him as much as he wanted her. And yet he thought of all her previous refusals and needed to hear her correct them. To take back her *nevers*. That choice he spoke of before.

"Say it," he commanded.

Her eyes widened, but she didn't flinch or pull away. Her eyes dazed with passion, her fingers digging into his shoulders. The color high on her cheeks. There was nothing else in his world except her.

"Yes, Frediano." Her breathing hitched, but she never looked away, never took her hands off his shoulders. "I want you. I want this."

He knew she was not experienced, and though need

and lust drove him, wracked him, he was gentle as he entered her. Made her *his*.

Mine. Only mine.

She stiffened, though she did not push him away or make any sound of distress. He kept himself still as he willed her to relax with his palms, his mouth. He sucked her nipple deep into his mouth until she let out a low moan. Slowly the tenseness melted away from her, until it was she who moved against him, their breaths mingling in harsh exhales and shaky inhales.

He let her find her own pleasure for that very first. It was a masterpiece to watch. Until she was shaking, shuddering, coming apart around him. His name on her lips.

But that was not enough. Not nearly enough.

"Again," he growled. And this time he set the pace. To make her as wild and needy as he felt.

"Please," she gasped, meeting his pace with something fervent and wild herself. The spiky edge of everything that sparked between them, dark and light, good and bad. Until his control cracked, until he was as lost as she. Until she sobbed out his name, and his own release came in a roaring, desperate rush that left him weak.

In the breathless, shuddering aftermath, he knew he would never understand what had come over him. He dropped his forehead to hers, trying to find…some answer. But this had been more powerful and dangerous than simply raw lust. He'd always controlled that before. Ruthlessly. Carefully.

But she was…different somehow, this woman. She was…

His.

He gathered her up, and she held on as he carried her through the chalet and into an ornate bathroom, dominated by a large fireplace that was lit, and kept the room warm and steaming. The bath was large and he carefully lowered her into it.

She sighed as the warm water encased them, her arms still around his neck while he settled into a sitting position. She leaned her head against his shoulder and something overturned inside of him. It felt like a door closing.

Or opening.

"I had never understood why people would do such foolish things for a kiss or a grope in the dark," Ilaria said, sounding far-off and dreamy. "But I did not understand, I suppose, what it could all feel like. I do now."

"Such a compliment," he murmured.

She laughed and the sound warmed him as her body moved against his. He wanted her again with such a surprising bolt of need that his grip on her tightened. If she was uncomfortable with it, she did not express it.

"Did I give you what you wanted, Princess?"

Her misty green eyes met his. There was something searching in her gaze, but he did not know how to give her whatever mysterious thing she searched for. Still, she smiled. "For a start."

CHAPTER ELEVEN

ILARIA HAD SHARED a bed before. When they'd taken in the orphans after the mining disaster, she'd had to share her mattress with two little girls. Those had been long, uncomfortable nights—missing her father and her life before he'd died.

This was very different.

The bed was much larger, for starters. Comfortable, like the mattress back at the palace. Cloudlike and perfect, the sheets smooth and luxurious.

But the main difference had been that during the night, when she'd woken from a dream of Frediano's mouth on hers. She'd needed only to roll over, to touch him. And he had responded in kind. Allowing her to explore him in all the ways she hadn't thought to do the first time around.

He had made her say it—*I want you, Frediano*— again and again and again, until it seemed all she could think was wanting him.

But when she awoke this time, wanting him and reaching for him, he wasn't there. She blinked her eyes open and realized daylight was streaming in the large window on the exterior wall.

Where he stood, looking out said window, fully dressed. "Good morning," he offered, not turning to look at her.

"Good morning," she returned, perhaps a little stiffly as she pulled the sheet up to cover her chest. She hadn't really thought beyond sleep and passion to this moment of just…having to figure out how to navigate this new world they'd created when they'd given themselves to each other.

Worry began to dance in her stomach. Had he not enjoyed it? Was he so fine an actor that she had been tricked somehow? She didn't know the purpose of such a trick, but…

"There is a breakfast tray set up for you," he offered. He turned slowly, something stiff and formal about him. But he went over and grabbed the tray on the table. He carried it over to her and then placed it on the side of the bed where he'd once been.

There were bowls of fruit, a plate of pastries and assorted beverages. It was enough for ten people. She looked up at him, and still he had not returned her gaze. She didn't know what that meant, what any of this meant. She was uncertain as to how to proceed.

She could not regret—not fully. Last night had been…wonderful. It hadn't been about anyone or anything except them, and that was…

When his gaze finally landed on hers, those dark eyes flashed with heat as they had last night and raked over where she held the sheet, because he knew exactly and intimately what she looked like without it.

Her worry evaporated, because she could see his desire for her. If nothing else, he liked the way she looked as much as she liked the way he looked. Their bodies were compatible, and maybe that meant there was hope for the rest of them.

A strange turn of events, but she was determined to be an optimist.

"We have much work to do today," he said, though his voice was gruffer than it had been. "But I wanted to give you adequate time to rest."

"I feel very well rested," she returned, and took a piece of fruit and nibbled on it. She watched him tear his gaze from her and return it to the window once more. She did not know what to say, naked in his bed, eating a breakfast that should have been feeding an entire banquet hall.

Eventually he turned once more to face her, and his hands were clasped behind his back. He had what she would call his *prince* look on. One of careful detachment and quiet certainty—that whatever he said would be obeyed.

Wariness crept in, because she did not wish to *obey* him. She also did not wish to go back to the way they had been, forever arguing with each other. She wanted... something else. Something more like last night.

"I think it's possible we will make a fine team, Ilaria," he said in that careful way of his that reminded her of when he was around his grandfather. "You can help people in all the ways you wish, so long as you fulfill your duties as Princess. I will have a wife our people will love and my grandfather can respect. It need not be a prison sentence for either of us."

It sounded so reasonable, and so much like what she had decided. It would be making the best of the situation. If they could work as a team. If they could be kind to one another.

It did not have to be about love, and she'd never imagined love for herself anyway. Perhaps he was right, and this was not the nightmare it had immediately felt like. She could admit that she quite liked sharing her body with him. He had been right. Love did not have to factor in to the heat that erupted when they touched.

When he made her feel things with her body she did not know had existed. And perhaps... Perhaps there was room for something pleasant. Care, if not love.

She swallowed, because it felt like a gamble. It would require trusting him in some ways, when she was so sure she never would be able to. But she had already trusted him with her body, and he had delivered. Quite spectacularly. "I suppose...that would be an acceptable outcome."

He smiled, and he was quite handsome when he smiled. She could almost believe that this could...work. That things could be good.

Indeed, they *would* be good. She had only to decide it. And see it through. Like always.

She would miss her old life, but perhaps once they forged a partnership, she would be able to find a way to exist in her new one as well. She was a princess. Surely anything she set her mind to was possible?

So they spent the next few days with protocol lessons in the mornings. If Ilaria had one regret in life—aside from accidentally marrying this prince of course—it was that she had not been able to spend more days in the classroom.

Perhaps she didn't care what fork she chose to eat her dinner with, or what wine went with what course in the evenings when they practiced the royal dinner, but she was endlessly fascinated by history. By the balance of power. What people did with it. And didn't do.

So the lessons on tradition interested her even if the practice meals bored her. She found the line of the Vantonella throne oddly familiar. The history of one family, one place, stretching back a century or more.

"You know, in a very strange way, it is not all that different from the farm," she said as he traced the monarchs he insisted she should have learned in school that she had not.

Frediano raised one of his brows. "You are suggesting your sheep are the same as the citizens of Vantonella?"

She laughed. Because he was clearly offended by the comparison, but she thought it apt. "The farm came from my grandfather's grandfather's grandfather. Passed down to the next oldest son and so on and so forth. It is its own tiny kind of kingdom, kept in the family. Ruled by Russos. My parents were the first Russos to have only a daughter. I always thought it rather lucky I did not have to give my birthright to a boy simply because of something I could not control."

"Your birthright. And yet you have made it sound as if you had no plans to continue your line."

"I suppose that is the luxury of being a mere peasant. I did not have to think of bloodlines and citizens. It did not matter if it was my own child, or one of our orphans who would take on the farm after me. Only that they loved it as we had."

She thought of that love. Of what happened next. Vita was running the farm with aplomb. Every report she received said it was functioning like a well-oiled machine. It did not need her. No one there *needed* her.

She studied Frediano. He was so strong, so severe, but when he gave little glimpses into his childhood hurts… Well, maybe *he* could need her. Was that possible? It was a strange thought, but no stranger than bloodlines and the realization she was part of the Montellero bloodline now. That she would be expected to have children, who would then be expected to take on the crown someday.

"There have been so many Montellero sons. What is the law if…" She found it hard to say the words, though the possibility now existed. "…if we should have a daughter?"

The idea filled her with something she did not know how to untangle just yet. In many ways she'd been a mother figure to some of the orphans at the farm, but she had never given much thought to being a mother herself. It seemed strange and unimaginable, as she remembered nothing of her own mother.

But she…did not dread that outcome. The scary part of it all was, she rather liked the idea of having a child.

Their child. Like he had said, they could be a team. And in being a team, they could, hopefully, correct all the mistakes his parents had made, and even a few her own father and grandfather had made.

"When my father married, my grandfather enacted a change in the law," Frediano said, studying the book carefully. "The oldest child shall inherit the crown. If there is more than one, they have the option to pass it down to the next child if they so choose."

Ilaria looked at him, though his gaze stayed firmly on the books they were studying.

"That is a surprise."

"Why?"

"I have seen nothing of your grandfather that speaks to a man who would bend tradition in such a way. Who might even consider that any child could certainly be an heir regardless of gender or birth order."

"You do not know my grandfather at all," he said sharply. "The King you find so offensive yielded and appealed to my father in all the ways he could. He made changes and would have made more, but this was never what my parents wanted. They only wanted attention, so it didn't matter if my grandfather gave them all they asked for, they still weren't satisfied."

He held such bitterness toward his parents. She supposed it was no wonder. He had claimed relief when they'd died, which meant they had hurt him in many ways he'd likely never share with her.

And because she felt sorry for that boy, she let the subject drop. They would never agree.

Or perhaps you've been wrong about King Carlo.

Surely sex had addled her mind if she was considering that? She knew what King Carlo had done. Perhaps he had acted out of ignorance and that detachment, but this did not make it right. A king should care. A king should want to help his citizens always, but especially during tragedy. A smart king would never trust a man like Giovanni.

So they moved from their afternoon lessons to a hike around the mountains. A surprising suggestion from the Prince himself.

Out in the chilly air, Ilaria felt herself relax even more. Here in the mountains, she was safe and free. And Frediano let her bound ahead. Explore. He seemed content to watch her.

She stumbled upon a little alcove of rocks, complete with a sharp cliff wall. A faded outline of a bull's-eye could be seen on the flat surface. She looked back at Frediano.

He stood on a rock, tall and broad, the wind whipping his hair and yet it somehow never seemed out of place. Almost like he was a rock himself.

He nodded to the bull's-eye. "When I was learning to be a prince, my grandfather would give me a few hours in the afternoon to explore. He did not wish me to be afraid of the mountains, nor be cooped up like an animal in a zoo. We would hike, practice archery, do whatever I wished for a few hours. He wanted to give me a taste of freedom, so I would always know how to find it even amid the daily pressures of royal life."

She looked at the bull's-eye, then back at him. "Do you?"

"Do I what?"

"Ever go find that freedom?"

"This is one of my favorite escapes, but lately, no. I do not wish to leave my grandfather alone for long."

She picked her way across the rocky ground to stand below him.

"That's the second time you've made it sound like your grandfather's health suffers."

He stared down at her. She could not read him, but she suspected a million emotions swirled behind that careful mask.

"Come. We must go prepare for dinner."

She could have pushed the issue, but she sensed... It would be like poking her fingers into an exposed wound and she did not want to hurt him.

A very strange turn of events indeed.

"You love your grandfather very much," she said instead.

"He is my grandfather."

"I know. I understand. My grandfather raised me, too. He was always there. I don't know what I would have done without him. Perhaps we are more alike than we've believed up to this point, Frediano."

"Is that so, Princess?"

"No matter the reason, being raised by a grandparent is a different experience. They are older. At some point, younger than perhaps we are prepared for, we become *their* caregiver. Or feel we must repay them in some way."

He stared at her, an expression she'd never seen on his face before. Perhaps because it was an expression with no mask. An arrested kind of ache had settled into his dark eyes. "A debt," he said, so softly she almost didn't hear it over the lashing winds of the mountain around them.

Ilaria nodded, feeling an odd lump form in her throat. Because at times it had felt, no matter how her grandfather had loved her, that she owed him a debt for being there. Surrounded by so many children who'd been left with no one.

Had she paid that debt? She had nursed him as his health had failed. She had read to him in those long, terrible nights knowing he wouldn't make it. She had tried so very hard not to cry then—not in front of him, or the children. She had been strong, because of that debt.

But he was gone, and all that was left was how much she loved him and missed him. And apparently all those tears she hadn't shed last year when he'd passed.

"Do not cry, *tesoro*," Frediano said, his voice gruff, but not an order. Gently, he reached out and brushed the tears from her cheeks. He pulled her to him and pressed a soft kiss to her temple. An offer of comfort.

And she took it. She leaned into him and let him hold her. She even managed to smile through her tears. Because being comforted…was something new. And wonderful. Deep within Frediano, there had to be a softer heart then he let on if he would offer this.

And more than that, in the memory of how hard she'd held on to her strength in the face of her grandfather's inevitable passing, she understood that hard shell he put on himself. Because there was no one to give *him* comfort.

No one to give him love.

"Perhaps I understand you," she whispered. Because she couldn't quite find the courage to say it as certainly as she wanted to. Or to think too deeply on words like *love*. She couldn't even look at him. She could only keep her cheek pressed to his shoulder.

And feel.

When the tears had stopped, she forced herself to look up at him. She wasn't sure *thank you* was the right response, but she wanted to offer something. He did not cry, and his grandfather was still alive, but there were still hurts inside of him.

She wanted to comfort them, as he had comforted hers.

So she rose on her toes and pressed her mouth to his. Not in the same way she had during their wild, passionate night last night. This was about comfort.

And he did not respond with heat or passion, or even that lazy exploration they had both indulged in last night. No, this was gentler. There was something *soft* about it. Him. The cold mountain wind whipped around them, but he was warm. He was strength. He held her, but his hands did not wander.

When he pulled away, there was a beat of silence where they simply stared at each other.

"We must get back for dinner," was all he eventually said in that gruff voice she was coming to believe meant that deep beneath his masks there were emotions swirling.

He did not look away from her. He seemed almost

puzzled, but he simply took her hand and led her back to the chalet in silence.

They engaged in a long, boring dinner about silverware and when she could stand or speak to the people on her right or left. They followed this with another dance practice, which ended the same way as it had last night.

The routine went on for days in the exact same manner, and Ilaria found herself…comfortable. If she thought about it, more than comfortable. She enjoyed this. She was even learning to like her husband. He was a patient teacher, letting her retry things as many times as she wanted without ever acting annoyed. He was a surprisingly astute listener—never forgetting a thing she told him, no matter how minor. If she didn't eat something at a meal because she didn't care for the food, it never appeared again.

"Have you had a report from Vita today?" he asked, as he invariably did. And when she told him of the goings on of the farm, he listened. Asked more questions. As though he might actually *care*. "I do hope the ordered medicine arrived."

"Yes," she responded, watching him carefully as he ate. She had figured he would be bored by tales of sick sheep and leaky roofs, and maybe he was, but he always sought to be part of the solution to the problem.

Again, something she understood. For he might be demanding and cold, but he was not a selfish man. Everything he did was not for himself—but for his grandfather or Vantonella or even now, sometimes, for her.

And it was that realization that had slowly began to

change Ilaria's feelings for him, though she could not explain it or fully understand it.

Sometimes she thought their nights together must have altered her brain chemistry in some way. Its own brainwashing. But each night she was so thoroughly pleasured she found she didn't mind it. She'd never had any idea that sex could *mean* something, could become so all-encompassing.

Tonight they lounged, naked and sated, in the gigantic bath. A fire crackled across from them, and outside, the stars shone in a dazzling array that *almost* matched the beauty of her husband.

And he was beautiful. In these nights, she saw the warmth in him. The man behind the self-restraint. He didn't offer much, no matter how she poked and prodded, yet she was beginning to put together the pieces of a man who existed under all that tightly wound control.

She still didn't understand his choices and what drove them, but she understood the harsh facade and that need to dominate came from a traumatic and cold childhood.

She had asked him about it, over and over again, as they'd studied the history of his family, but he had given her no more than the history books. No reason behind his father's rebellion, no understanding of his grandfather's cool detachment. He was as opaque as the factual tomes meant to preserve Montellero history for the centuries to come.

A history she was part of now. A humbling thought, perhaps made even more humbling by the fact that she and Frediano alone knew that it hadn't meant to be *her*.

"Frediano… You have such a dim view of love and marriage. Why did you seek it out in such a way? You needn't have married *that* night."

If he found her question odd, he did not show it. He considered the dark night outside the windows. And did not look at her when he finally spoke. "I had a plan," he said, opaquely. A nonanswer she knew she would have no luck getting behind. But she was learning to ask different questions, to circle around that which he did not wish to share until she could unearth it by surprise.

"Why did you want to marry Sophia, specifically?"

There was a pause. She'd asked him many questions he'd refused to answer, and she suspected this one to be the same. Maybe she even hoped it, because part of her didn't want to know.

Part of her had come to see him as hers.

He shrugged. "She was simple. She would have known what was expected of her. She likely would have demanded nothing, and your uncle would be forever under my thumb, and I could've made sure his family stayed in line."

She studied the planes of his back as she soaked in those cold words. So detached. But she was beginning to see the different layers of him. The way he pulled back when he sought control. The way warmth and kindness could pour out of him when he let it go.

She understood he preferred the control. It felt safe to him, because it was what his grandfather clearly prized. What she did not fully understand was his devotion to the man beyond a *debt*.

"And what have I demanded?" she asked.

He turned to her, his eyes tracing the lines of her body until she shivered, knowing what came next after that dark, dangerous stare.

Somehow things were changing, and she had never known how to fight change. It swept in and did its will, and you could only ride out that storm.

She'd long thought Frediano a storm, but all those consequences she'd imagined were not this. Not coming to care for him, wanting to understand him. Not hoping she could find some way to help him open his heart.

To her.

"I thought you wanted nothing, Princess. But to help."

"I do want to help," she said, and this time she did not mean only those less fortunate. She meant him, and that wall he had built around himself to protect a wounded heart.

She slid onto his lap, wrapping her arms around him as she took him inside of her, as had become habit. Habit and joy. Want fulfilled.

He'd asked her what she wanted all through this, and in a million ways he'd shown her just how right she'd been to want to explore the desire between them, but maybe he'd also shown her there was nothing wrong with wanting something for herself. For wanting more than what was on offer.

If she could be a princess who helped people, a woman who enjoyed her lover, a potential mother, why couldn't she be a wife who loved her husband—and have him love her back?

His gaze held hers, but she saw that wariness in him.

He desired her, and she thought maybe he'd even come to *like* her, but he didn't have to say that which she already knew.

He would never love. He didn't know how. But he had compassion. He had held her when she'd cried. In some ways, he understood.

So maybe she could show him how to love.

The days were coming to an end, and Frediano found himself dreading a return to the palace. He enjoyed each part of his day here. Waking up to Ilaria, sharing breakfast and history lessons with her. Watching her frustration—that he'd once felt many years ago—over the complex rules of a royal dinner. And most surprising of all, it was not just the nights of pleasure with her he looked forward to. It was their afternoon walks.

They were dangerous, he knew, that first day he'd nearly told her about his grandfather. A secret he could never trust her with until there was no hiding it.

Then she'd cried, over her own grandfather, and he'd felt something shift inside of him—much like their first night together when she'd leaned her head on his shoulder. He did not understand these shifts, the gentleness they seemed to pull out of him. He certainly didn't trust them, and if he was a smarter man, he would not continue with these hikes.

Still he engaged because she…was that freedom he'd spoken of.

He watched her now, climbing gracefully over a boulder before she tilted her head back to the sun. She smiled as the wind teased over her face. She took such joy in so many things.

Back at the palace, she would not be free to tip her face to the sun. They would be under constant scrutiny. There would be no impromptu lovemaking in an open field.

A dark pain twisted inside of him at the thought. He did not wish to take her back to where she might be unhappy. But when had her happiness come to matter? The point of this was not *happiness*. It was understanding her, so he could control all outcomes.

He *had* succeeded in that, but he had let himself become too comfortable in this little fantasy world he'd created to win her over. Part of him insisted he should pull back, but a larger part of him figured they had such little time left he might as well enjoy it.

She made an odd noise, and then he saw her tumble.

He rushed over, but she was laughing, sitting there between rocks, her hair and clothes disheveled. "Just lost my footing," she said cheerfully, her cheeks an alluring pink and her mouth curved in a sweet smile.

But she *could* have hurt herself on these jagged rocks and uneven terrain. Perhaps she was used to it, but he could not stand the thought of her injuring herself out here.

"You must be more careful," he said, scowling at her as he held out his hand to help her up. But she was already getting to her feet on her own, brushing her palms on the pants she wore. She smiled up at him as she noticed his hand, and then took it though she no longer needed the help or the leverage.

She was holding his hand as she moved forward. A casual, intimate gesture of something…far softer than desire. Something that slithered through his chest and threatened to do…something to him. He did not know what.

Ilaria squinted up at the giant peak in front of them. "Will you tell me about it?" she asked gently.

"About what?"

"What happened when your parents died." She gestured to the peak above them. Not Monte Morte, but certainly similar.

"What happened is of no consequence," he said stiffly, because he could all but see it in his mind's eye. His mother's tumble, the muffled, echoing scream because she'd been too far away to reach, but not far away enough to mistake what had happened.

"I think it is of some consequence," Ilaria continued, using that carefully neutral voice she was learning to employ so well. "And it seems there is more to it than the history books would tell us. Perhaps it would behoove me to know, so I never say the wrong thing about it if asked."

She was smart, his wife. He had noticed over the past few days that she did not plod on headfirst when she did not get the answer she wanted. She watched, she waited, she rephrased, reshaped until she had gotten the information out of him he hadn't meant to give.

"Perhaps I can even use it," she continued. "If I know what happened, I can always present myself to the press in a way that sounds nothing like them."

It was a good reason, it appealed to his fears. She

knew what she was doing, and so he should not allow her this win. But...

He wanted to give her what she wanted. In this last day before they had to leave. Maybe this too would anchor the obedience he needed from her.

But that didn't mean he had to give it to her all in her way. "I suppose it is a good conversation to have, as when you produce heirs we will have to be on the same page about their upbringing and how that is portrayed."

She blinked. She did not move forward now, but she did not drop his hand. She stood on a small rock so they were more eye to eye than usual when they were on even ground. "You could say *have children*, Frediano. Not *produce heirs*. We aren't creating them in a science lab."

"No, indeed we are not."

Her cheeks pinkened prettily at that and he wished to change the subject to more pleasant things, but she would not let this line of questioning go, so they might as well finish it.

"As with everything, we will endeavor to appear as different from my parents as possible. They did not like to leave me with nannies. It was bad for the image of being boldly anti-royal and oh-so-common man, you see. But they didn't particularly want me around. They liked to dress me up, teach me funny things to say that might get a laugh from their friends, but they didn't want to have to worry about if I was fed or well."

Her hand tightened around his. A squeeze of comfort. He looked at their joined hands and tried to understand what this woman had done to him.

But understanding did not matter. Only control did.

"We will have nannies, of course, but our children will know us both. They will have a traditional upbringing, so they are ready to take on their duties as they age." He looked around the mountain field where they stood. He could almost picture these phantom children. With her eyes and her smile, enjoying the nature around them as she did.

"And they must know they are loved and never question if they will be taken care of," Ilaria added, making the pain in his heart shove deeper and deeper.

"If you like," he said, and it sounded choked even to his own ears.

"I do. Now, your parents…"

"They liked outdoor pursuits. They were young, athletic people who needed to move, to be involved, to be paid attention to." He looked up at the mountain peak again. "They liked free-climbing. It was dangerous, exciting, and people loved to praise them for it. Exclaim over the danger and ask them about their experiences. Monte Morte was off-limits, of course, and so they simply *had* to do it."

"A foolish risk," Ilaria said. She slid off the rock and surprised him by reaching out to put her hand over his heart. "When they had a son who needed them."

He laughed. Bitterly. "Need them? Everything I was then and am now was in *spite* of them. They sat me at the base of the mountain, then began their preparations. I was to stay where I was until they returned. They had provided me with snacks and blankets. A few books and toys. It was more than they usually thought to remember for my care."

"You were *there*?" Her eyes widened and there was such shock, such horror. He had never spoken of this with anyone. Even his grandfather—because his grandfather had been the one to find him, so he had not needed to speak of it.

But Ilaria's hand on his heart, her soft gaze and the… It wasn't pity, or maybe it was, but whatever it was in her eyes felt tender and warm. It felt like reprieve, and he was powerless not to try and find more of it.

"I saw my mother fall," he said dully. He could see it so clearly, no matter how many years past. Sometimes he woke in the middle of the night, breath clogged in his lungs, that image replaying itself over and over again.

"Frediano." She sounded so anguished for him and he…

He was a grown man. Not a boy. He needed to pull himself together. "I did not see my father, but somehow I knew he had fallen as well. At first I tried to get to them, but I got so turned around and night descended. The snow was unforgiving. I was lost. I was quite certain I would die. Three days I was out there."

Her fingers curled in his shirt. It was so odd. She hadn't known his parents, she barely knew *him* and yet she seemed to care. This information seemed to hurt her somehow, when back at the palace it had only ever been a secret to be carefully guarded.

To be forgotten.

And for good reason.

"But it was my grandfather who found me. Not an aide, not a volunteer mountaineer. My grandfather." He looked at her then, held her gaze. Some part of him needed her to see, to understand. "He dug me out of the snow. He carried me to safety. And when all the stories came out about my parents' tragic and untimely death, he did not use the papers to avenge all they had done to him. He hid the fact I'd been left alone, allowed Vantonella to grieve the tragedy without adding their poor choices to the mix. He allowed me months to recuperate, to prepare outside the spotlight. He gave me time."

Her eyes had filled with tears. For him. He did not know what to do with such emotion.

"He would not be a very honorable man if he used the press to avenge the wrongs done to him by his dead son," she said, her voice cracking with those unshed tears.

"That is the first nice thing you've said about my grandfather."

"Perhaps…" She swallowed. "Perhaps I have misjudged him."

Skepticism at her easy capitulation lowered his brows. "Perhaps you have a fever."

She laughed, though she still looked sad. "He has still made mistakes, but we all do." She stepped forward and leaned her head onto his chest next to her hand over his heart. "He has made you feel as though your behavior is a condition of his love. That control is more important than anything else. Perhaps in these circumstances I can even understand you both felt this was the only way to deal with what happened with your parents. I understand your devotion to him now, but there is one thing he did not give you, and there is one thing you need."

"And what is that, *tesoro*?"

He wished he could keep her here, with the warm sun above them, the mountain air around him. Her leaning into him, as if he mattered to her at all. But her next words froze him from the inside out.

"Love."

He stiffened. That word. Love would be the end of his control, just as it had once been the end of his grandfather's. And Frediano could not risk it. *Love* would be the end of everything he wished to accomplish in order to ensure his grandfather lived to see another year.

"There will be no love, Ilaria. I have no use for it."

She lifted her head and stared at him, without saying anything for the longest time. As though if she stared long enough, she would be able to see through him into the depths of his soul.

But hearts and souls were uncontrollable, irresponsible things, and he had no desire to trust his. "Come. We only have one more practice here before the royal wedding dinner on Saturday. And it must go perfectly."

She nodded, never looking away. Never dropping his hand. Yet when she spoke, her voice was cool. Detached. "Yes, Your Highness."

It should not hurt. It *did* not hurt.

He wouldn't allow it to.

CHAPTER TWELVE

ILARIA HAD SPENT the remainder of the day feeling battered by the terrible reality of Frediano witnessing his parents' death, nearly dying himself, and the resulting trauma he clearly refused to acknowledge.

He had chipped away at all the defenses and prejudices she'd had against him, until she was nothing but a heart that hurt for him—for what he'd endured as a boy. That was not loss. It wasn't even tragedy. It was neglect and abuse on top of a tragedy.

No wonder he held his grandfather in such high esteem. The King had literally saved his life, and so Ilaria found herself softening to the man as well. Surely he was not all that wrong and bad if he'd done the things Frediano relayed?

But that did not make him right or good. King Carlo had not given that boy what he'd desperately needed, so now as a man he did not know how to accept it or give it.

And somehow she found herself, in all the ways she'd thought she never would, loving this man. A prince. The grandson of the King she had spent the past decade cursing.

But people weren't their families, their crowns. They were the complicated mess of choices they'd made. Because life was always a choice. For princes and peasants alike.

And she understood his. They really weren't all that different. They had both sought to control what they could in their worlds, but she had always had love, someone to turn to, someone to protect or believe in. Even that debt she'd felt to her grandfather had not outshone the love she'd felt for him or received from him.

Frediano had only had duty, and she thought he had the potential to be so much more, have so much more if he learned to trust in love. She wanted to be the one who gave this to him. Needed to believe she could.

And if you can't?

Her chest ached at the thought, but was this not just another storm? She could wait for it to rage, then clean up the mess it left behind. She had to believe she was strong enough to give this to him…because no one in his life had been.

Being strong for others wasn't just who she was, it was how she expressed her love. Sometimes that was sacrifice—like accepting she would be leaving her farm and life behind and taking on a life completely out of her realm—but sometimes love was simply…believing.

After dinner, she had meant to avoid the dancing lesson. To go to her own room alone, to find the space to figure out what loving Frediano meant, what choice she'd make in lieu of that realization, but instead she found herself dancing with him, following him to bed, and turning to him, again and again, in the night.

Wordlessly seeking some answer to the questions that plagued her.

When she woke the next morning, there was no breakfast waiting for her. No husband. Only an outfit carefully laid out on the chair by the window.

She sighed. The honeymoon was over. In more ways than one. But she had choices. She could yell at him, of course. She could demand this, that and the other.

But Frediano prized control, and so she would use that against him.

She got dressed, found Frediano's aide waiting for her out in the living room surrounded by glass and the mountains.

"Your Highness." Eduardo bowed. "Your things are packed and on the plane. The Prince is waiting for you, whenever you are ready."

"Thank you, Eduardo," she said, smiling warmly at him, though she felt anything but warm.

Frediano was already on the *plane*. It felt like a slap, but she was also growing to understand the man she loved. He wanted control in all things, and clearly at least part of his control was difficult to hold on to when it came to her.

So he had separated himself. Protected himself. She would take this as a win instead of a hurt.

She followed Eduardo to the car, then took the silent drive to the small airstrip, formulating her own plan. Because no doubt Frediano had spent the morning formulating his.

Eduardo led her onto the plane, and Frediano was indeed already there. There was a laptop and a stack of newspapers on the little tray beside him. He was freshly shaven, looking sharp and forbidding. He did not look up from the phone he held in his hand.

"Good morning, Princess," he greeted.

"Good morning, Your Highness," she replied demurely, hoping her lack of reaction might surprise him enough to look at her.

He did not.

So she settled herself into a seat across from him. She entertained herself for a while watching the plane take off. She did enjoy flying. She never would have known, if not for him.

She had determined she would not speak first and was in fact keeping track of how long it took him to speak. It took nearly an hour—so long she'd considered breaking her promise to herself. But he'd eventually broken, though he spoke in that bored, royal tone she didn't like.

"At the royal dinner tomorrow night, I will put you in touch with Signora Costa. She will assist you in whatever patronages you wish to aid. All that you desire to accomplish should be within your reach, so long as your royal duties do not suffer. You can help whomever you wish."

"And if I wish to return home?" she asked, casually.

"All trips must be approved by me and my staff, but you should be able to spend as much time as you wish in Accogliente, within reason."

He did not look at her. He read his phone. Like he had flipped a switch and turned back into the man he'd been before.

But it was a mask. And she had the means to get under it.

"Will you accompany me on these trips home?"

"If it improves our image."

Image. Masks. *Duty.* Things she could not care about when she wanted to get to the heart of *him.* Her next words made her stomach flutter, but she still had to say them. "And if I'm already with child?"

There was a pause, and she was studying him closely enough to see that his fingers tightened ever so carefully on the phone. He shifted, almost infinitesimally. "We have a doctor on staff."

"Important, obviously, but I meant more in terms of what we discussed yesterday. You said you had no use for love, but you will love our child, will you not?"

Still he did not look away from his phone. "No doubt you will be enough for whatever children we have together."

"And that's it?"

"What else would there be?"

"Something more than the robot your grandfather has built himself into." She struggled with her temper now. She could not expect a man to be changed overnight, but she supposed she was selfish enough to wish she was enough to change him. "Being a detached automaton is not something to aspire to. I know you prize control, but—"

"Control is everything, *tesoro.* You would do good to take that lesson on board as we return to the palace. Every aspect of your life will be scrutinized, and you

must be above scrutiny if you wish to continue the mon-
etary disbursements to your little farm."

She had forgotten about his bribe, because she had
come to care for *him*. So much so that those words hurt.
She knew they were meant to and she struggled to keep
that from having her reacting. But she did not have the
control he did. She didn't *want* it. "You only prize control so much because you never have had any."

He lowered his phone, fixing her with one of those
cold stares she remembered from the first days. How
had it all changed so much, so quickly? "Do you think
you know me, just because I lulled you into a sense of
security to teach you the ways of the palace? Do you
fool yourself into thinking you understand me? I assure
you, you do not."

It took her a moment, longer than it should have really, to fully understand his meaning. He was claiming
he'd spent the past week tricking her. She supposed she
should have felt some pain. Some betrayal. A terrible
kind of shock.

But he'd made a grave error, because she had always been good at reading people. And no amount of
his amazing control could stop her from understanding
what this was. What he was trying to do.

So she laughed.

Frediano jolted at the noise, looking at her with a
startled frown. It occurred to her then that he *believed*
the little stories he told himself. She supposed that was
why he was so good at control.

Denial.

"Yes, you have fooled me, Frediano," she said, and

still she couldn't quite keep the laughter out of her voice. "Acted and lied. And so effectively!"

"Your sarcasm is not lost on me."

She leaned forward. "You can lie to yourself, Frediano, but your body does not lie, and your eyes do not lie. You care for me, against all that well-trained control. Perhaps it is not love, you would have to let go of fear to love me, but it is more than an act."

His gaze remained cool, but there was the flash of *something* before he looked back at his phone. "You may think whatever you wish, Princess."

And he did not speak to her for the rest of the flight, even as they deplaned and were ushered into the palace. Still, he was with her as she walked to her rooms.

He stopped in front of the door, waved the palace staff away. Once they were gone, he looked at her and she thought perhaps he'd say something meaningful. Kiss her.

Or maybe that was wishful thinking, because his body and hers had never been complicated.

"It will not be appropriate for us to share rooms here," he said instead, following the words with a bow. "I will see you at dinner with my grandfather this evening." He turned on his heel and marched away.

She was almost too stunned to speak.

Except to call him a coward as he walked away.

Frediano heard her accusation but chose to ignore it. Like he'd ignored her words in the plane. Her *words* didn't matter any more than her feelings did.

He had no feelings.

All that mattered was his plan.

He took care of some of the business affairs he'd put off while he'd been gone. He double-checked on some of the plans for tomorrow's wedding dinner. He watched the clock as he had an afternoon meeting with his grandfather before dinner.

Frediano had much to do, and absolutely no room to think about Ilaria.

Except as he stood watching the clock, he could not seem to push away the realization that he felt *lonely* without her by his side. Because her presence was warmth. Sunlight. Her passion contagious—not just for what they could find together, but for everything. Helping others. Her farm. Flying. Hiking. She *enjoyed* the world around her.

And he did the same when he was with her.

She had not reacted to his withdrawal as he'd expected. At all. From the many times she'd turned to him in the night, to her careful questions on the plane, to her *laughing* at him. As if she did not believe the honeymoon had been anything more than a carefully executed plan to get what he wanted.

Perhaps he had grown a little distracted, had allowed himself a little too much personal enjoyment, but he'd gotten what he wanted, hadn't he? She'd softened toward him. She'd shared his bed. She'd learned the protocol and even on the plane ride had given the perfect performance of a dutiful princess.

She might even be in love with him, which would allow him a certain amount of sway over her. Always. Just as his grandfather's love for his son had twisted and turned Carlo into changing laws, into bending over backward, into his physical heart giving out because his emotional heart was so burdened.

But the bitter thoughts did not take root as they usually did. Instead, Frediano found himself standing there, thinking of Ilaria climbing those rocks, her laughter on the mountain winds.

This was unacceptable. There would be no more spending time by themselves. He'd gotten what he wanted, and now there would be space. And soon he wouldn't think of her at all.

Frediano assured himself of this, over and over, as he strode through the palace to his grandfather's office. When his grandfather's aide ushered him inside, Frediano was surprised to see his grandfather already sitting. The pale pallor of his face immediately set Frediano on high alert. He looked at the aide, who did not meet his gaze.

"Grandfather, are you well?"

"Merely a little tired." Carlo waved his concern away. "Tell me, how has your wife fared?"

"She will behave impeccably tomorrow night, I can assure you. She wishes to begin charity work almost at once, which will fit into the image she gave at our introduction. I will introduce her to Signora Costa, and Noemi will work with her to make sure the press covers her endeavors in a respectful manner that meets with your approval."

"This sounds quite promising."

Frediano had planned to once again bring up his grandfather's potential stepping down, but there was something about the man that seemed particularly frail today, and something was wrong with Frediano. Because instead of forging ahead and doing what needed to be done, he excused himself.

He motioned for his grandfather's aide to follow. "Has the King seen his doctors?" Frediano asked once they were safely in the hall.

"He was having some pain," the aide said in hushed tones. "We brought the doctor in Wednesday. He urged surgery. The King refused."

"I told you to inform me of any and all changes in his condition," Frediano returned between gritted teeth.

"Your Highness…" The aide cleared his throat, clearly uncomfortable. "My instructions were to inform you of any changes when you called for your check-in. But we had not heard from you since Tuesday, and your grandfather did not wish you to be bothered."

Frediano did not move. He held himself completely still. But inside something had detonated, an odd ringing in his ears as everything inside him crumbled.

His entire adult life had been in service to his grandfather. Had been the repayment of a debt. And it had only taken her a few days to ruin him completely. It didn't even have to be love. Ilaria had swept in and upended every last plan. Every last inch of himself.

And who had suffered? Not Frediano, but everyone around him. Ilaria had lost her home. His grandfather was losing his battle with his health. All because Frediano had let himself be distracted. By his own selfish wants and desires, while his grandfather suffered.

It was unconscionable.

His hands curled into fists, his only reaction to the aide's words. Ilaria had said that love was sacrifice, but all love ever seemed to do when he touched it was sacrifice others. Ruin things, blast in and create wreckage wherever it went. As if there was no escape from his parents' legacy.

Frediano had failed. In all ways.

But his grandfather would not sacrifice for him. Ever again.

CHAPTER THIRTEEN

Ilaria DID NOT see Frediano again. Noemi came that night and told her the King wasn't feeling well and there would be no dinner. Ilaria didn't know how to feel about this. She doubted Frediano would be quite *so* cowardly as to fake an illness for his grandfather, and there had been those times Frediano had mentioned Carlo's health.

Cryptically, in that wounded way of his that had kept her from poking at it. Perhaps something serious with Carlo's health made him stay away from her.

Or perhaps he was just using whatever suited him as a reason. This seemed just as in character.

She considered going to Frediano's rooms despite his clear declaration they would not share one. She had few doubts they would end up in Frediano's bed if she did.

Perhaps that was why she didn't do it. Being intimate would not solve the problems between them. Frediano needed to be ready to discuss what he felt, and that was not something that would happen overnight.

Her team was in her room early the next afternoon, all abuzz about preparing her for the royal wedding dinner. She had requested the jeweled gown from that first day. She knew Frediano liked the way she looked in it, and she planned to use that to her advantage.

She was nervous, she could admit that as she looked at herself in the mirror. She looked like someone else and would be expected to behave like this someone else. In front of so many strangers.

You've studied and practiced, she reminded herself. And if it was only about not embarrassing herself, she likely would have felt more calm. But she found herself…wanting to make Frediano proud.

Even if that made her a fool.

Once she had been molded and painted into what felt like someone else entirely, she could only stand and stare at her reflection, waiting for Frediano to arrive to escort her to the ballroom.

She breathed, as he had taught her at that first public appearance on the balcony. In, one-two-three, and out. She focused on her breathing to distract herself from her nerves, trying to not think of the audience she would be on display for. And when Frediano finally arrived, dressed in a crisp black tuxedo, she smiled at him. Her handsome husband. So tall, so stern.

He did not meet her gaze, instead looking somewhere just beyond her. "You look lovely," he said. Rotely. He offered his arm.

Ilaria took it. There was little else to do. He said nothing as he led her into the ballroom. Offered no advice or reassurances as the palace staff prepared for their entrance.

Something…had changed yet again. His mood was different. He seemed so withdrawn, so harsh.

"Is everything all right?" she asked.

"What wouldn't be?"

"Your grandfather. Is he feeling better?"

Frediano's mouth flattened, and she hadn't thought that possible. "It is time to enter, Princess." He led her inside the grand room, already full of people.

Ilaria's nerves threatened, as they had when she'd stepped onto that balcony. So many eyes. So many people. But this time she was prepared. And she wanted to impress her husband, so he could see.

She could be everything he needed.

She greeted everyone as they were introduced to her. She curtsied, smiled, and tried to get to know each of her guests. There had been little biographies on all of them that they had studied back at the chalet, and those had been like the history. Far more interesting than correct napkin usage.

She had always liked people and talking to others helped ease her nerves as well. She liked understanding, helping. And people, in turn, had always confided in her. Her grandfather had always told her she had a knack for getting people to spill their guts.

Frediano introduced her to Signora Costa as he'd promised, and the older woman seemed excited to have the Princess's support, so Ilaria enjoyed spending some time with her talking about the charities already in place, and how they could expand the organizations.

"Perhaps you can convince that husband of yours to make his charity work more widely known."

Ilaria stared at the older woman, who seemed to read her surprise and tutted.

"He gives his time and money generously and in equal measure but is always so adamant about keeping it out of the press. But if we could advertise more of his efforts, I'm certain we could convince others to give as well."

Ilaria understood then, on a painful little jab, that in his constant efforts to be the opposite of his parents, he kept even the good he did hidden away. All out of fear.

When he came to her side once more, he behaved like a perfect imitation of King Carlo. Detached. Not seeming fully present. She began to worry about him, but worry for her husband was washed away when her uncle was announced and brought forward, with her aunt on his arm.

For a moment Ilaria forgot everything she'd been taught. Everything she had practiced. A hot, painful wave of rage went through her.

If not for *him*, her father would be alive. If not for *him*, she would be home on her farm. If not for *him*, everything would be different.

"Now is not the time, *tesoro*," Frediano whispered next to her.

She hated that he was right, but she was gratified to see *some* flash of the Frediano who had a beating heart. His hand was firm on her back, and his gaze on Giovanni cool but not fully detached.

Frediano smiled down at the couple. "Giovanni. Mrs. Avida. You grace us with your presence this evening."

"I'm sure you'll have a few moments so we can talk

privately," Giovanni said. There was a pleasant enough smile on his face, but when he flicked a glance at her, his eyes were full of hate.

Ilaria's plastered smile became more genuine. She wanted him to hate her as much as she hated him.

"I do not know that I will," Frediano returned smoothly. "This is not a business dinner, Giovanni. It's a celebration of my marriage. To your *niece*. Which is why you received an invitation."

It was a surprising little slap-down. So surprising Ilaria could only stare at Frediano. He gave no indication that he'd done anything special, but she knew that protocol dictated he be slightly more polite than *that*.

"I'm so happy for you, Ilaria," her aunt said. She opened her mouth to say more, but Giovanni's glare had her shutting it and looking down at her feet. They were ushered into the dining room so the next couple could be announced.

Ilaria and Frediano were finally escorted into the dining room. She tried not to grimace when she realized she'd be sitting next to her uncle.

"Sit. Eat. Be merry," the King said from his spot at the head of the table. Ilaria noted he looked a little pale. Perhaps he really had been ill last night. Perhaps there was much more going on than she realized.

Frediano pulled out her chair, and Ilaria sat in it, just as she'd been taught. Then the rest of the gathering took their seats.

She looked at her plate, called back on everything Frediano had taught her. She ate with the right utensils. She smiled and spoke when spoken to and endeavored to make her husband proud. She even ignored the fact her uncle sat next to her.

"King Carlo, you always host the most delicious dinners," Giovanni said, overloud to Ilaria's ears after he'd scraped his plate.

"Thank you, Giovanni," the King returned. Ilaria watched him. Carlo smiled. He spoke with what could only be called friendliness, but there was no warmth behind his words, his eyes. She had always imagined the King and her uncle were great friends, laughing at the lowly commoners they exploited and did not care about.

But Ilaria began to wonder if the King showed that he cared about *anything*. One way or another.

"I suppose you are in the way of family now," the King continued, taking a sip of wine. He made a strange move, almost like a wince. As if he was in pain. Ilaria looked at Frediano to see his expression even more closed off.

"I like to think so," Giovanni returned. He reached over and put his hand on Ilaria's shoulder, bringing her attention back to him. He gave her what she supposed looked like a friendly squeeze.

But it *hurt*.

She looked at Frediano, whose eyes were hot on Giovanni's hand on her shoulder now. He even began to move, as if to remove Giovanni's hand himself. But this would be a disaster, she knew, for so many reasons.

So she stood—Giovanni's hand having to fall off her by her sheer force of movement. "Will you all excuse me for just a moment?" she asked, careful to keep her voice soft and demure and her smile easy and even. "I'll be right back."

She slipped away from the table and then out into the hallway. She'd go to the bathroom. She couldn't put cold water on her face because it would ruin her makeup, but she could take a few moments to breathe in quiet.

She did so, finding the bathroom empty, which allowed her the space and time to try to ground herself. But as she looked at her unfamiliar reflection, she thought of how she missed the chalet, almost as much as she missed her farm. She did not want this glamorous life. She did not want a life of pretend, and yet...

She loved her husband, and if love was sacrifice...

She would sacrifice for him. Because underneath all his issues was a man who wanted to do good. Do the right thing. Like her father and grandfather had been. In her experience, there had been no men in power who had been interested in what was *right*.

But Frediano loved his country and wanted to do right by it. Oh, he had some warped ways of going about it, and he was still controlling in his way. But...

He wanted to *do* good, and if he worked through some of his trauma, perhaps he could even allow himself to believe he *was* good. Good enough to love and be loved.

And with all that love inside of her, she felt strong enough to return. To face the people, and her uncle, and anyone who dared cross her and her husband. She stepped out of the bathroom and into the empty hallway.

"Ilaria."

The sound of her uncle's voice startled her as much

as the fact he stood just opposite the bathroom. As if he'd been waiting for her.

His expression was smug, his color high as he'd likely had a little bit too much wine with dinner. He was a short man, no taller than her, but he was wide and had spent a lifetime learning how to intimidate with his size, if not his height. Ilaria struggled not to shrink back.

"You will pay for what you've done to my daughter. One way or another."

"*To* your daughter? Don't you mean *for*?" Ilaria returned, chin raised. She put every effort to sounding as calm and disdainful as her uncle. "I saved her from your schemes. Your unfeeling treatment of her."

"Schemes that would have seen her a princess, wealthy and powerful. Something you have always claimed to be so disdainful of, but you wear that expensive whore's gown. You share the Prince's bed."

It hurt, when it shouldn't. But there was a kernel of truth to his words. She had not *wanted* to be royalty, but she hadn't tried to escape, had she? She'd taken the bribes or blackmail depending on how you looked at it, and she had, in fact, shared the Prince's bed. She stood here in an expensive gown she would have been contemptuous of just days ago. She'd sipped wine and learned etiquette.

She was a hypocrite.

"I did not take you for a scheming slut," he said conversationally, that pleasant smile on his face completely incongruous to the words, but he grabbed her arm and squeezed tight, pulling her closer as he hissed out the next words. "At least you were smart enough to bag a prince, unlike your stupid whore of a mother who would only spread her legs for a *farmer*."

She made a noise. She could not have characterized it—some kind of pained growl or groan of outrage and disgust and *fury*. She wrenched her arm out of his painful grasp and raised her hand. So consumed by hate she didn't fully realize she'd meant to slap him until her uncle smirked and tutted before he jerked his chin to the side.

There Frediano stood, observing, that cold, icy scorn on his face. Her hand hovering there in the air, no way of excusing what she'd been about to do as *anything* other than strike her uncle.

In the palace. During the royal wedding dinner he'd been so adamant go well, with his grandfather's health in a questionable position. With press running about snapping publicity photos and such.

She'd lost her control, and she knew this was something he would not forgive.

Frediano was so consumed by rage that his vision had hazed. He held himself still because if he was within touching distance of Giovanni Avida, he would tear the man from limb to limb.

And they were in public. Though this hallway seemed to be deserted, just beyond those doors was half of Roletto. He needed to somehow, someway, restrain himself.

But the man had put his hands on his wife.

"Princess," Frediano managed without sounding as enraged as he felt. "Perhaps you'd like to drop your hand."

And his wife stood there, hand still raised, staring at Frediano as though *he'd* been the one to hurt her.

So many things rolled through Frediano at once he could not make sense of any of them, except that he could not stand his wife within reach of her vile uncle.

He moved, barely feeling his body. Barely seeing the world around him. Because his vision was just a replay of Ilaria jerking her arm from Giovanni's angry grasp. Ilaria defending herself, because Frediano had not defended her.

Frediano came to stand next to Ilaria. He put his hand on her back. Her spine was straight, her shoulders back, but there was a slight tremor there, too.

He turned his gaze to the man Ilaria hated so, and Frediano hated him, too. With a boiling, blinding fury that eradicated all good sense. That stripped his composure until there was next to nothing left.

"Giovanni," he said. "If I ever see your hands on my wife again, you will no longer have hands." He delivered this statement as someone might have said, *I prefer chicken to salmon.*

Clearly, it surprised Giovanni, who he stood there, gaping like a fish. "What did you say to me?"

"You heard me. Now I suggest you leave my sight."

"I am your grandfather's Minister of Energy. How dare you—"

"I am Prince Frediano Montellero of Vantonella and twice I have seen you manhandle my wife. Consider this a very gracious response."

"She is *my* niece. You were supposed to marry *my* daughter."

"Perhaps you should have treated your daughter better. Perhaps we both should have. But she is happy now, and I will ensure she remains so. As I will ensure Ilaria has everything she wants. Now, I will give you one last opportunity to leave properly."

"Properly? After you broke promises to me? *I* will ensure the press knows exactly what kind of man you are, Frediano. And as for your *wife*, this lying, Accogliente trash…"

Frediano did not hear the rest. He saw Giovanni's hand begin to reach out—whether to point or grab or do *something* in the general vicinity of Ilaria, it did not matter. Frediano stopped it.

With his fist. Smashing firmly into Giovanni's face. The man stumbled back on a primal scream, and Ilaria made a noise of surprise as well.

But he did not care. He only cared that he had stopped that horrible creature from ever putting hands on his wife again.

Ilaria tugged at his sleeve, and he realized dimly she'd been doing so for some time now. "Frediano…"

But now he heard it. The telltale click of photographs being taken.

And his life being ruined…at his own hands.

CHAPTER FOURTEEN

TIME SEEMED TO speed up. Suddenly there were aides and guards whisking the photographer away, taking Giovanni out of the room while blood spurted from his nose, and Frediano standing in the midst of it all, his hand still curled into a fist. Staring at the spot where Giovanni had once been.

Ilaria was likewise frozen. She did not quite understand everything, but she understood enough that Frediano did not view this as a triumph quite the way she did.

"Your Highness," Eduardo said, his eyes wide as he wrung his hands together. "It is time for the dance."

Frediano finally straightened. When he turned toward her, his gaze was cold. Empty. "Are you all right?"

She blinked at him. She thought…there was some concern there…deep down. But mostly she could not tell. He was a cold ghost of himself. "Yes," she managed.

He held out his arm and she took it, feeling almost as robotic as he acted. All the shock and adrenaline was leaking out of her and she didn't know how else to reclaim this moment.

Now they had to dance in front of everyone. While palace staff scurried about and whispered in corners, Frediano led her to the dance floor.

It was the strangest moment of her life and she didn't worry about the steps, her uncle, the press. She worried about her husband. He was so stiff. So gray. So *broken*.

He had once claimed princes did not break, but she knew somehow she had brought upon his downfall. He said nothing, but she watched his face. He'd lost control. For her.

She leaned closer and spoke to him in a whisper no one would hear. "Frediano. Surely you can explain the circumstances to the photographer and—"

His words were quiet but flat in return. "The circumstances do not matter. They want a story and I gave them one. Our aides will try to stop it, and they will fail. I have failed."

Her heart broke for him. That even now, in what was a terrible moment, there was no emotion to be found in those words. "Frediano. Look at me."

He did, met her gaze with nothing but King Carlo's practiced distance.

"We can fix this. Together. I promise," she urged. "People make mistakes, and that was… Perhaps it was a mistake, but is it really so awful that you defended me? *Us?*"

"If I had controlled myself, no, it would not be. But I did not. So that incident, like everything else that has involved you, will be wreckage."

This hurt, and she could not excuse that hurt away on his trauma or his obsessive need for control. She swallowed at the lump growing in her throat. "I see. It's all my fault."

"No, it is mine. I made all the mistakes from the start. So now, I must fix them." He swept her around the ballroom until she thought she'd be sick. Until she thought she'd begin crying right here in front of everyone.

"There is only one thing to do," he said, each word grimmer and more detached than the last. "You will go back to Acclogiente. There can be no divorce, but we will live our lives as separately as possible, without the press finding out."

She jerked in his arms. "What?"

But he only continued. "You will stay there and have your life back. Except when absolutely necessary, we will not have any contact."

She could not wrap her mind around this bizarre change. Could not come up with words. The music ended and he dropped her hand. He bowed and she knew she was supposed to curtsy, but she could only stare at him. He gave her a pointed look and finally her knees bobbed in a terrible approximation of a curtsey.

This was the end of the event for them as he led her out of the ballroom. But he immediately dropped her hand and began to stride purposefully away.

"You cannot simply…" She ran after him, scurrying in front of him and standing in his way. "You cannot just…command I go back and that be it."

"But it is it," he replied, sidestepping her. Or trying to, but she merely leaped into his way again.

Finally, *finally* some emotion flashed in the depths

of his dark eyes. "You have ruined all my control. And as long as you are near, I will lose it, again and again, until we are all nothing but wreckage, and I will not stand for it. I will not."

She reached out for him, but he moved back so she found only air. "What is between us does not have to be wreckage," she said, and knew she sounded desperate. But if this was not a time for desperation, she did not know what would be.

"Then what would it be, Ilaria? What could it possibly be?"

"It could be love, Frediano," she said, and maybe there were tears in her eyes or on her cheeks, but all she could really seem to grasp was that he was shaking his head.

"Those are the same things to me. Do you not see what I have done?"

"You have stood up for me. You have cared for me. And in doing so, allowed me to do the same for you. Do you think because your parents did not—could not—love you, or that your grandfather is so bad at showing it, you are not *worthy* of it?"

"I am the Prince of Vantonella, *tesoro*. I am worthy of most things."

She felt a mix of despair and temper and let them both echo in her voice. "That is an evasion and you know it."

"But this is not. My role, my only role, is to keep my grandfather *alive*. Perhaps if you understand that, you can understand why we must handle things *my* way."

It was a dig, but pain and hurt did not well up inside

her. Instead, the thought of him losing the one person he seemed to care about had her soft heart hurting for him. "Frediano. What do you mean?"

"My grandfather has several blockages in his heart," he said. His words were calm, sharp, but his eyes were wild. "He can live with them, for now. But all doctors advise he have surgery to remove said blockages. They have told him stress and the demands of his schedule are not tenable. I assured him I would marry acceptably, with no scandal, no shades of my parents' mistakes, so that he could step down and attend to his health. I thought your stunt at the introduction to the public would kill him then and there."

It was a barb, and it hit home. But… "It did not."

"No, it did not. My behavior, in front of all and sundry this evening, did everything you did not. He will see my father's irresponsible behavior stamped on me, and he will not step down, and his life will be cut short. Because I could not control myself."

"It is not your job to control yourself to save him, Frediano."

"You of all people would tell me it is not my job to save someone?"

He had an unfortunate point, but she saw that only as a sign… He understood her, too. Because deep down, under all his fear, he loved her, too. "You can help people, but you cannot make their choices for them. You cannot—"

"In this instance, I make all the choices. You will go home, Princess." Finally, his eyes met hers and there was something almost soft there. Almost…regretful. "Go back to the life you loved."

It was alarming how little she wanted that now. It hurt, beyond telling, that things had changed so irrevocably. Because she didn't want to go home. She wanted to be by his side. "But I love you."

"And I do not love at all," he returned, then turned on a heel and strode away.

Frediano didn't wait to be summoned to his grandfather's office after the dinner. He simply waited.

It was hours—no doubt Carlo was busy doing damage control—but Frediano did not move. He stood outside the hall and stared at the office door and felt nothing.

Nothing but the hollow, echoing failure of ruining everything he'd tried to build. Essentially sentencing his grandfather to death, all for a little personal vengeance.

When his grandfather finally arrived, it was with two aides in tow. One carried a stack of papers.

"Come," was all King Carlo said as his assistant opened the door. Frediano followed his grandfather inside.

The aide spread out the printouts of the online newspaper stories, updated in real time. Frediano was surprised to see a picture that did not feature him and his fists. Instead, it was a picture of Ilaria and Giovanni, Giovanni's hand curled around her arm in an aggressive manner.

Even now, the tide of rage swept through him and

he had to hold himself very still not to leave this very office and hunt Giovanni down.

"Frediano." His grandfather's voice sounded exhausted. "You have behaved as your father would have."

Frediano's head jerked up to look at his grandfather, his king. The only person in his life who had ever helped him. It was the cruelest cut his grandfather could have made. Frediano tried to weather it, but his eyes closed against his will.

"I can only apologize for the damage I've caused, Grandfather," Frediano managed to choke out. Because there was no way to fix this. He had behaved as his father would have.

"I would prefer if you take me through the events of this…altercation," Carlo said. He pointed at the paper with the picture of Giovanni and Ilaria. "There are conflicting stories here, and it is best I know the truth so we can decide what to do about it."

Frediano did his best to recite the pertinent facts without emotion. Giovanni's unacceptable behavior towards Ilaria, yes, but he also did not sugarcoat his own mistakes. "Unfortunately, I lost control when he attempted to touch Ilaria again. I punched him. Once."

If the man hadn't fallen backward, he would have likely done it again.

King Carlo was silent, looking at the printouts and tapping his finger against his desk. He sighed. "I suppose you have done the honorable thing, then."

Frediano was sure he'd misheard. "What?"

"Even if he is my Minister of Energy, and her uncle, you could hardly let him treat your wife in such a manner. Perhaps I wish you would have used your words, but I think we should be able to limit the damage." Carlo nodded, then gestured for the assistant to take the papers away.

Frediano was speechless. He kept expecting his grandfather's wrath...only to have Carlo excuse his mistakes. Forgive them, even. Much like the one after the announcement when Ilaria had given her unsanctioned little speech.

His grandfather had not condemned him. There had been no criticism. No recriminations that he had chosen poorly, that Ilaria had done badly. Frediano had expected those things, but instead the King had always twisted the events into a positive.

Frediano thought back to what Ilaria had said. Not that his grandfather didn't love him as his parents hadn't, but that his grandfather was so bad at *showing* love. He did not wish to believe his grandfather bad at anything, but he realized...

Ilaria had been a mistake he'd made from the first, and at every turn his grandfather had tried to make it okay. The one time he could not—this very public disaster—King Carlo was still not blaming him as Frediano had feared. Carlo was disappointed with the situation, yes, but was seeking to solve it.

He had not raged. He had not stripped Frediano of his title. Yes, he had compared him to his father, but then he'd swept the mistake away. As he had always done.

Only Frediano had never realized that in itself was a gift. Maybe even...an expression of his grandfather's *love*.

It shook him, and he tried to deny it, but Ilaria's voice was in his head. And perhaps…he was just as bad. Just as incapable.

But Ilaria had shown him…

"I sent Ilaria away. I thought it best if we maintain as much distance as possible. She much prefers the country."

Carlo looked up at him. "She is your wife."

"Yes." His wife. Who had said she loved him.

Loved him. She'd wanted to stay, and he'd sent her away because… It was a shock to realize all the ways she'd been right. Her love terrified him, so instead of dealing with it or her, or his own feelings, he'd sent her away.

So he could have control. So he could protect himself.

But no matter where she was, the feelings were there. He looked at his grandfather, needing that…guidance. "But I…fear I may love Ilaria. I have let my guard down. I have protected her and forgotten my duties. It is best for the crown if I…if I create the distance that will allow me to…" Frediano had not stumbled over his words this way since he was a boy.

"Love is nothing to be feared," Carlo said, seeming confused. "I quite loved your grandmother," he said, gesturing at the royal portrait behind his desk.

It was something of a shock to hear his grandfather speak of *love*. Of the late Queen at all. "You never speak of her."

"I suppose because…" Carlo studied the portrait, and Frediano saw something strange in his grandfather's gaze. A wistfulness. "I miss her every day. She was my heart. My balance. But I lost her, and then I failed your father in trying to make it up to him. Perhaps I have failed you, too."

"Failed me? You saved me. I have never thanked you for all you have done for me, Grandfather." That debt even Ilaria understood.

Carlo looked at him now, both confusion and that failure he spoke of in his dark gaze. "I tried to love you differently than I loved your father. I hoped to fix my many mistakes of overindulgence and the excuses I made for him. You are so respectful and such a good man, I thought I had succeeded." His grandfather paused, taking a breath that worried Frediano by how labored it sounded. "If you feel the need to thank me, I have failed you. There is no 'thank you' for love. You are my grandson, and you owe me nothing."

Frediano did not know how to take on this information. They had never spoken like this. Never would have...if Ilaria had not introduced the entire notion of love in the first place.

Carlo eased himself into the chair, looking tired and gray. Worry twined with love and confusion and all the mistakes of the past few days. But he saw something in this moment that he had not seen before.

Maybe his grandfather still refused to step down because he saw only duty.

Not love.

"You have never failed me, sir," Frediano said, endeavoring to sound strong. Because the love he had for his grandfather was that strong. "You have given me everything. And the choices I made…" Frediano struggled to deal with all the mistakes he'd made.

He'd made. Because it was not his grandfather's fault that he had seen love as a weakness. Frediano had chosen control, as Ilaria had once accused, because he'd had *none* before coming to the palace.

These were his own failings. And his grandfather had always taught him to own up to his mistakes. To learn, to change. And watching his grandfather clearly struggle with his health in *this* moment, Frediano knew he had to push forward. Even at this worst possible time.

"I think it is time to explain myself more clearly about my wishes for you to step down."

Carlo's face hardened, but Frediano did not let it stop him. If this was about love, not duty or control, then all that mattered was expressing that love. "It is not that I want to see you step down. You are a fine king, and I wish our country could enjoy your leadership for many more years. But personally and selfishly, I do not wish to see you die so soon, when you could spend many more years in my presence, and in my future children's presence. I would like them to know the kind of man their great-grandfather is from experience, not my memory."

For the first time in his recollection, Frediano saw true reaction from his grandfather. And it was utter shock. But Carlo did not send him away or mount an argument, so Frediano continued.

"I do not wish to be King for the sake of being King. I wish you to take care of your health. I wish *you* to be all right."

There was silence in the aftermath, as Carlo slowly got a hold of his expression and returned to one of calm detachment.

"I will consider all you've said, Frediano," Carlo said. This would usually be where Carlo dismissed him. Instead, the King stood and crossed to Frediano and put his hand on Frediano's shoulder. "You are a credit to me, Frediano," he said. "And you will be a fine king."

Frediano felt his throat constrict. "Because of you, Your Majesty." And Frediano bowed to the man who had given him love, even though Frediano had not always seen it.

Then, once King Carlo dismissed him, Frediano finally understood what he must do.

CHAPTER FIFTEEN

ILARIA COULD HAVE fought the guard who'd taken her back to Accogliente. But she didn't. She had seen the man she loved broken, and she did not think staying would fix it.

So she arrived home to the farm that was home and now felt strange, hugged everyone tight, and then spent the night in her old room, in her old bed, alone and miserable.

It didn't seem fair in the least. This man she hadn't even known last month had swept into her life and up-ended it, changed her irrevocably inside and out, and then sent her away.

He had ruined her life in every way possible, and she'd simply let him do it.

No. She sat up in bed, having slept no more than a few small snatches. It was later than she usually got up, the sun streaming in the windows of the cottage. She blew out a frustrated breath. Her eyes were puffy, her head achy, and everything felt *wrong*.

So you must right it.

She *always* righted wrongs. She charged in and

solved problems, fixed mistakes, patched up holes. Frediano had been hurt last night. Why hadn't she stayed to mend the hurts? Why hadn't she fought for him when he was at his lowest?

Why should she treat him any differently? Simply because he was a prince?

Well, *she* was a princess now.

She was the one who understood love, so she would have to be the one to fight for it.

She got dressed quickly, then rushed outside. Everyone should be out in the fields at this hour, so she went in search of someone to give her a ride to the train station.

She climbed the mountains of her home and did not feel quite the same old wave of comfort. Oh, she still loved this place, and hoped to bring her future children here for romps among the sheep, but her home had become her husband.

The man she loved and needed to save. When she finally caught the first sign of someone in the distance, she stopped short. This man was tall and broad. His dark hair windswept, and even from the distance she knew.

He was here.

For a moment she only stared. There were a cluster of sheep around him, and he was standing with one of the younger boys, Roberto. But when he straightened, unerringly looked over to her, she felt compelled to move forward.

Before she reached him, he leaned down and said something to Roberto, who scurried off. The boy sent her a jaunty wave as the young sheep bounded after him, but then they were gone.

And it was just her and Frediano. He had begun to walk toward her as well until they met on a patch of grass, separated by a small boulder.

When he finally walked close enough he would be able to hear her over the howling wind, she spoke. She pointed to the two little sheep who found him a curiosity and had followed him.

"They like you."

He gave them both a supercilious stare. "All my dreams have come true," he returned dryly. "Sheep like me."

"Why are you here?" she asked him, because he was so *controlled*. So him. This did not feel like the precursor to anything she wanted.

"You need ask?"

"Yes, I do. You sent me away just last night. Assumed our lives would be lived apart. You told me you could never love. And now you're here."

He reached out, touched his hand to her cheek. "Ah, *tesoro*. I have come for you, because there is *only* you."

Her heart leaped at the words. He moved around the boulder until he stood in front of her, so tall and sure and…

Different, she realized. There was something different in his face, something different in the way he spoke to her. There was…warmth.

"Last night, I spoke with my grandfather. I felt as though I'd failed him, as though I owed him, and he…

felt that he had failed me. He informed me that…there is no 'thank you' in love."

She looked up at him, wanting to wrap her arms around him and hold him close, but also needing those words she so desperately wanted to hear. So she held still. "For once I agree with your grandfather."

His mouth curved. A real smile. The kind she thought she'd never see on his face.

"It was your words in my head. Changing the way I saw everything. Him. Myself." He brought his other hand up to hold her face there. "You have taught me to look beyond the walls I erected for myself. To be brave enough to see that…all those feelings I viewed as the enemy, the ones I tried to lock away deep inside are a strength I did not know I possessed. And I always considered myself quite strong."

It surprised a strange little laugh out of her, something almost like a sob. He pulled her closer, into the circle of his arms, and his gaze never left hers. Dark, demanding but…not cold. Not this time.

"I was *afraid* of love. What it looked like, what it meant. I thought it would be wreckage because it wrecked my grandfather, and I thought what I felt was out of control, and perhaps it is, but sometimes control doesn't mean what I thought it did." He looked into her eyes. "I cannot give you all the freedom you deserve. A divorce will simply always be out of the question. But I can give you as much as possible. Whatever you wish. I will sacrifice all I can."

But in his words, in his gesture, she realized… She'd

been wrong, too. "Maybe we were both wrong, Frediano. Because I don't want you to sacrifice for me."

"And I do not wish you to sacrifice for me, *tesoro*."

"So maybe...it is balance. Maybe it is giving," she said, touching her palm to his chest. "And receiving," she said lifting his to hers.

"Leaving here would be a sacrifice for you."

"Staying would be as well. Because I love you, Frediano. I love the man you are when you let yourself listen to your heart. I want to build a life with you that exists...in that balance. We will both sacrifice, because we love. And we will both not want the other to sacrifice, for the same."

"I love you, Ilaria," he said, with the hushed reverence those words deserved, even with the mountain wind whipping around them. "I wish never to be apart from you. So we will be together. We must spend most of our time in the capital, but we can summer here. We will raise our children to know this place as well as the palace. We will have a true marriage, and love, and when the time comes, you will make an admirable queen. We will build a life together. And if there is wreckage..."

"We will have to repair it. Together," she said through the lump in her throat. Because it was beautiful.

He reached out and smoothed away the tears that had fallen with the backs of his fingertips. "Oh, Ilaria, my love. I promise to give you everything in my power, and that is quite a lot."

"Yes, it is. But I only want your love, Frediano. That will be enough for me."

He pulled her against him, his mouth a whisper from hers. "It is yours," he vowed, as her arms came around his neck out in the wild mountain winds. As his mouth touched hers under the warmth of a morning sun. "Forever, Princess."

EPILOGUE

LOVE DID INDEED change everything.

King Carlo stepped down to have his surgery and Frediano and Ilaria became the much beloved King and Queen of Vantonella, known for their efforts to aid those in need, particularly children.

They also thrilled their people and the press and the former King by having five children of their own—each more stubborn and strong-willed than the last.

Something Frediano could not deny as his five children stumbled inside after spending the afternoon roaming the mountains of Accogliente with *sheep*. He had insisted on building a house on the farm that would fit all of them so his children could know something of their *Russo* kingdom.

He surveyed his children. They were dirty and disheveled. The knees of Russo's pants were torn, the sleeves of Carlotta's shirt ripped. Pigtails had come undone and young Vinnie even sported a bloody lip.

Frediano looked over at his wife. "Wreckage," he muttered darkly, but he returned the grin she sent him. "I'm not sure you predicted quite *this* much."

"No, but we keep cleaning it up and repairing it all the same."

"That is because we are so good at it."

"Indeed."

And so that was what they did. Cleaned up the children, ate dinner with everyone who worked the farm these days as was tradition in the summers in the mountains. Sometimes, the former King even joined them and could be found some mornings walking the mountain paths with an errant sheep at his heels.

But tonight it was just Frediano and Ilaria as they told bedtime stories, tucked in wiggling children, scolded and offered I-love-yous in equal measure. And when they retired to their own room, Frediano took his queen in his arms.

"Your children will be the death of me, *tesoro*," he said, nuzzling his mouth into her neck until she sighed the way he liked best.

"And you love it," she replied, laughing as he tumbled her onto the bed.

For a moment, he surveyed her, marveling as he often did about the twists of fate that had brought him his heart. He looked down at her, those green eyes as bewitching as they had been all those years ago. "I do. I thank you for showing me that I could."

And then he showed her, as he had many times before and would many times going forward, just how deep his love went.

* * * * *

If you fell in love with
The Prince's Royal Wedding Demand
make sure to watch out for debut author
Lorraine Hall's next story for Presents,
coming soon!

#4081 REUNITED BY THE GREEK'S BABY
by Annie West

When Theo was wrongfully imprisoned, ending his affair with Isla was vital for her safety. Proven innocent at last, he discovers she's pregnant! Nothing will stop Theo from claiming his child. But he must convince Isla that he wants her, too!

#4082 THE SECRET SHE MUST TELL THE SPANIARD
The Long-Lost Cortéz Brothers
by Clare Connelly

Alicia's ex, Graciano, makes a winning bid at a charity auction to whisk her away to his private island. She must gather the courage to admit the truth: after she was forced to abandon Graciano...she had his daughter!

#4083 THE BOSS'S STOLEN BRIDE
by Natalie Anderson

Darcie must marry to take custody of her orphaned goddaughter, but arriving at the registry office, she finds herself without her convenient groom. Until her boss, Elias, offers a solution: he'll wed his irreplaceable assistant—immediately!

#4084 WED FOR THEIR ROYAL HEIR
Three Ruthless Kings
by Jackie Ashenden

Facing the woman he shared one reckless night with, Galen experiences the same lightning bolt of desire. Then shame at discovering the terrible mistake that tore Solace from their son. There's only one acceptable option: claiming Solace at the royal altar!

HPCNMRA0123

#4085 A CONVENIENT RING TO CLAIM HER
Four Weddings and a Baby
by Dani Collins

Life has taught orphan Quinn to trust only herself. So while her secret fling with billionaire Micah was her first taste of passion, it wasn't supposed to last forever. Dare she agree to Micah's surprising new proposition?

#4086 THE HOUSEKEEPER'S INVITATION TO ITALY
by Cathy Williams

Housekeeper Sophie is honor bound to reveal to Alessio the shocking secrets that her boss, his father, has hidden from him. Still, Sophie didn't expect Alessio to make her the solution to his family's problems...by inviting her to Lake Garda as his pretend girlfriend!

#4087 THE PRINCE'S FORBIDDEN CINDERELLA
The Secret Twin Sisters
by Kim Lawrence

Widower Prince Marco is surprised to be brought to task by his daughter's new nanny, fiery Kate! And when their forbidden connection turns to intoxicating passion, Marco finds himself dangerously close to giving in to what he's always promised to never feel...

#4088 THE NIGHTS SHE SPENT WITH THE CEO
Cape Town Tycoons
by Joss Wood

With two sisters to care for, chauffeur Lex can't risk her job. Ignoring her ridiculous attraction to CEO Cole is essential. Until a snowstorm cuts them off from reality. And makes Lex dream beyond a few forbidden nights...

YOU CAN FIND MORE INFORMATION ON UPCOMING HARLEQUIN TITLES, FREE EXCERPTS AND MORE AT HARLEQUIN.COM.

HPCNMRB0123

Get 4 FREE REWARDS!

We'll send you 2 FREE Books plus 2 FREE Mystery Gifts.

FREE Value Over $20

Both the **Harlequin®** Desire and **Harlequin Presents®** series feature compelling novels filled with passion, sensuality and intriguing scandals.

HARLEQUIN
PLUS

Try the best multimedia
subscription service for romance
readers like you!

Read, Watch and Play.

Experience the easiest way to get
the romance content you crave.

Start your **FREE TRIAL** at
<u>www.harlequinplus.com/freetrial</u>.